THE OMENS CALL

A HORROR ANTHOLOGY

DANIEL WILLCOCKS

JULIE HINER

OTHER TITLES BY DEVIL'S ROCK PUBLISHING

Novels

When Winter Comes (Collected Edition)

Serial Fiction, "When Winter Comes"

The First Fall (Episode 1)

Buried (Episode 2)

Black Ice Kills (Episode 3)

Masks of Bone (Episode 4)

Into the White (Episode 5)

Winter Comes (Episode 6)

Anthologies

The Other Side: A Horror Anthology

Keep up-to-date at

www.devilsrockpublishing.com

For the good, the bad, and the ugly omens.
No matter your shade, no matter your color, your message is
heard.
Shine your light.
Show your path.
Guide the weary souls home.

We create our own omens, I think, and then mystify
ourselves trying to understand their significance.

— Steven Trust

FOREWORD

Omens are a language, it's the alphabet we develop to speak to the world's soul, or the universe's, or God's, whatever name you want to give it. Like an alphabet, it is individual, you only learn it by making mistakes, and that keeps you from globalizing the spiritual quest.

— PAULO COELHO

When I was fourteen years old, I stood beneath a blackening sky and watched the roiling clouds approach.

Five minutes prior, I had been playing football in the playground with my friends, scraping knees and pounding Lucozades. Lee was taking a swipe at Rory's shins, Matt was showing off his running speed (what would you expect from a kid that was already over a foot taller than the rest of his peers), Sarah and Alley were sat on their jumpers and giggling about something that only they knew had happened, Ry was... Well, we never really knew what Ry was doing.

Then the sun vanished.

It wasn't a slow process. I blinked and it was gone. Day to night. Summer to storm.

Three hundred kids ran for cover as the first droplets of rain fell. The sheet of rain could be seen in the distance, approaching like a thick shower curtain of misery.

Yet, there I stood. Watching and waiting.

An electricity filled the air. God's stomach rumbled, and in that moment I felt something larger than myself. An omnipresence that couldn't be described in words, but could be felt in flesh.

Droplets the size of marbles turned my skin to goose-flesh. I didn't put my jumper on. I stood there, absorbing the brunt of the storm's spray as my white school shirt turned see-through. I remember shouts behind me, though I don't know the words that were spoken, my mind fixed to the sky at the strange black cloud passing before the colossal char-coal clouds.

The birds flocked overhead, an artistic murmuration swelling and shrinking as they fled the worst of the coming attack. Light flashed in the distance, though still far enough away that I couldn't see the lightning. Their silhouettes spiked temporarily, leaving an intricate afterburn behind my eyes.

The birds knew.

The birds understood.

The birds warned others away.

They say that in every living creature are segments of invisible code, instructions to detail the path to survival. The jackrabbit knows to flee at the snap of the twig. The Retriever knows how to sniff an approaching attack of epilepsy on its human companion. Wild creatures know to clear the area before a thunderous rumble of an earthquake or the first sniff of ashen smoke from the birth of a forest fire.

And then there are the omens.

The pre-warnings written in the scripture of the Earth.

The harbingers of bad tidings.

For some, they may be simple. Black cats, tea leaves, and interpretations of symbols in the condensation that drips down a broken window. For others, they may be larger. The swirling waters of the altering riptide, the sudden appearance of a hundred cats sitting on your garden fence…

… or the approaching storm.

I didn't know what message the sky was sending me that day. Even as she held my clammy hands and drew me tight to her, I had no idea what the next few days would bring. My girlfriend stood beside me, marveling at the clouds, her breath catching as static turned our arm hairs to sentinel soldiers. She laughed. Giggled.

The sky replied with gusto, roaring its warning at me.

The teachers on duty ushered us inside.

We stalked back to class, smiles on our lips, the rain hissing behind.

We went to our separate classes.

I shivered at my desk alone.

A forewarning of times to come.

She dumped me the next day.

I'll never forget that day. Its crystal clarity inside my head is startling. I remember each breath, each beat of moisture, every frozen polaroid moment standing in that shower. The palpitating beat inside my chest.

I was fourteen years old when I received my first call from the omens.

They told me of approaching misery.

That a young boy was about to receive his first heartbreak.

Or, at least, that's how I chose to interpret it.

Seems too specific to be coincidental, don't you think...?

Daniel Willcocks

August 28th 2021

THE OMENS CALL

EVERYTHING AS IT WAS

BY WARREN BENEDETTO

First published in "Night Terrors Vol. 1" by Scare Street, 2020.

When I first walked into our crooked two-room house, Mama was standing at the sink, staring out the window at the barren fields outside.

The wind was blowing steadily, sending great big clouds of dust swirling through the air. It made a shushing sound against the glass, like someone was asking for quiet. There weren't any crops in our field, or the next field, or the next... or any, it seemed like, for as far as the eye could see. With nothing in its way, the wind just blew and blew forever, right through Oklahoma and into infinity, carrying all the dirt along with it.

I stood behind Mama and watched as she wiped a plate with a dishrag, round and round and round, real slow, like her mind was somewhere else. After a while, I opened my mouth to try and say something, but I couldn't get any words to come out. I guess I made some sort of noise though, because Mama turned around real quick. I must have spooked her. She dropped the dish onto the floor, where it shattered into a thousand pieces. Her face went sheet-white.

"Anabel," she whispered.

She put her hands over her mouth, then took a step closer to me. Her eyes got wet. She reached out and touched my cheek, then my hair. Her hand was shaking. It was like she was testing that I was real, that I wasn't some kind of ghost or apparition. Finally, she dropped to her knees and hugged me so hard I thought my ribs would break.

I put my head on her shoulder and let her hair tickle my nose. I could smell soap on her neck and sweat in her hair. Smoke, too. She wasn't supposed to have cigarettes—Papa said it made her smell like an ashtray—but I knew she kept a few rolled up in the bedrail, along the side of the mattress. She'd sneak a quick puff or two out on the back step some-times when Papa wasn't around, blowing the smoke side-ways into the wind, then snuffing the cigarette out on the side of the house and tucking the leftover stub into the seam of her apron.

Mama hugged me for what felt like forever. Finally, she pulled away and held me at arm's length, her hands still on my shoulders. She touched my cheek again.

"Glory be," she said. "My baby's home."

Mama hadn't changed much since I'd last seen her, though I'd be lying if I said she didn't look older. I wasn't sure how long I'd been gone—six months? A year?—but her hair seemed grayer than I remembered. Her skin was looser around the eyes too, with dark circles, real puffy, like she'd been crying a lot. I suppose maybe she had been. Times were tough. Real tough.

Of course, the first thing she said when she saw me, after she caught her breath, was to tell me that I looked a fright, and to set about fussing with my hair. Appearances had always been so important to her. Even though we didn't have much, she always found a way to look nice. Hair done up in curls, lipstick on her lips, everything clean and tidy. She was a real looker, is how Papa put it. Used to be, at least. He'd say that second part with a wink, and Mama would snap him in the rear with her dish towel and say, "Dale! Stop teasing!" Then later I'd see her in the mirror, pulling at the skin around her mouth, trying to make the lines go away. They never did, for long.

After she swept up the pieces of the broken plate, Mama took my hand and walked me into the bedroom.

"I made a new dress for you," she said. "For when you came home." She opened the bedroom closet and rummaged around inside. "Papa said I was wasting my time, that you weren't ever coming back, but I told him, I said, 'My time's my business, and yes, she sure as heck is.' He wasn't too happy with that." She laughed. The sound was sharp and loud in the tiny, low-roofed room. "You know how he feels about sassing back."

Did I ever. If there was one thing Papa hated, it was sass. There wasn't any place for a girl to be talking back to her father. Or her husband. Or any man, really. Not unless she wanted a handprint on her hide. I learned that lesson the hard way. Only had to be taught once, though. Papa made sure of that.

"I prayed on it, though," Mama continued. "I prayed on it really hard." She pointed behind her at a small table by the bed where she had set up a photo of me, along with some melted-down candles, a handmade cross, and a small jar full of dirt. "I prayed that you'd come home, and the crops would come back, and everything would go back to how it used to be. And now, glory be, here you are."

I walked over and picked up the photo. It was a picture of me and Charlie Henderson from next door, taken by Papa at the Church of God Easter Festival a few years back, before he had to sell off his camera to pay for groceries. We were five, maybe six years old, both clutching these huge jackrabbits and looking just happy as could be. A big banner sagged over our heads, with the words 'HE IS RISEN' painted on them in bright red letters.

I remembered that day so clearly. The sky was blue. The wind was still. There wasn't any dust. We weren't sick yet.

It was a good day. Maybe the best.

Maybe the last.

PRETTY SOON AFTER THAT DAY, the dust storms started. "Black blizzards," people called them. They'd come across the sky like a towering black ocean wave, as far and high as the eye could see, just waiting to crash over us and wash us clear off the Earth. Except, instead of water, these waves were made of dirt. When they hit, the dust was so thick that we could hardly breathe. We couldn't even step outside without a wet towel over our faces, lest we take in too much dust in our lungs.

Mama said the storms were an omen, that God's wrath was upon us because we were losing our faith. But Papa saw it differently. He saw it like God had abandoned us. All of us, all at once. We were forgotten by God, forgotten by the government, forgotten by everyone.

"A man has to make his own way now," was how he put it. "We're on our own."

I remember Charlie's dad, Mr. Henderson, answered "Amen" to that. That was a church word, which I thought was a funny thing to say to someone doubting God. But maybe that was the point.

Before long, people started getting sick, coughing, spitting up black phlegm. Dust-sick, they called it. Babies and old people had it the worst. It got the Miller twins down the road first, one then the other, a few days later. Then it took old Mr. Kleffman, and also Mrs. Robinson from the grocery in town. Soon, even strong men like Calvin White and Tom Frantz were laid up, their breathing sounding like rusty nails in a shaken tin can. Not everyone who got dust-sick died, but the ones who didn't coughed so bad, they wished they would've.

While we were hunkering down during one of the storms, I asked Papa why everything had gone so bad so quickly. He said we were in a depression, and nobody could fix it, not even Mr. Roosevelt. That made me scared because, if the president couldn't fix it, who could?

I wasn't expecting an answer, but Mama gave one anyway.

"The Reverend," she said.

Papa snorted out a bitter laugh, then spit into a jar. "Some reverend. Man ain't even got a church."

Papa was right. The Church of the Resurrection was nothing more than an old tent with a bunch of wooden benches and a raised-up stage in the front. The Reverend preached from behind an altar made of bushel baskets, with an old door laid across them. That was part of what Mama liked about him though. He didn't need a big building like the Church of God did.

"It means he's humble," she said. "He's regular, just like us."

"Humble ain't got nothing to do with it," Papa grumbled. Mama opened her mouth to object, but Papa kept going. "Just look at him. Regular folks ain't got suits like that. That's a city-made suit. Naw, he's a huckster, through and through. He just likes the attention. Wants to hear poor folks clap for him, to hoot and holler and shout 'Glory be!' at whatever nonsense he's spewing."

We had started going to see the Reverend around a year before. Things were about as bad as could be for us at the time. First, we lost our crop, then Grandma got dust-sick, then Mama lost her baby right when it was ready to be born.

For a while, Mama couldn't even bring herself to get out of bed. She'd just lie there with the crook of her arm over her eyes, a handkerchief clutched in her hand. Nothing Papa would say could get her up.

It was Mrs. Henderson who said the Reverend could help. She had lost a baby too, and started going to see him soon after. She said he was really something special. Said he claimed he could do miracles. That he was our salvation. That he alone could save us.

After a time, Mama wasn't getting any better, so Papa took us to the Reverend to see what all the fuss was about.

He was a big man, the biggest I'd ever seen. His face was sunbaked, with light hair that flew around his head like a crazy halo when the wind blew. He always wore a black suit with a long red tie, no matter the weather. He was a sour man. Humorless. I never once saw him laugh, or even crack a smile. He showed his teeth, sure, when it suited him. But there was no joy in his eyes when he did. They were flat and black, and his smile was mean. Cruel. The kind of smile you'd see a man make when a cripple fell on the steps and his groceries spilled out on the ground.

You'd think a man as big as he was would have a voice to

match, but he didn't. His voice was thin and reedy. It seemed to come more from his nose than his mouth. The way he preached didn't sound like any preacher I'd ever heard either. The Mass we used to go to at the Church of God was quiet and reverent, with its hymns and homilies and silent prayers. The Reverend's Mass wasn't like that at all. In fact, he didn't even call it a Mass—he called it a Revival. It was loud and angry, with talk of demons and plagues and the Devil, of the End Times and the godforsaken ground. That's what he called it: godforsaken. Said Satan himself must've cursed the land for it to dry up like it did.

He'd get the congregation all fired up, to where they were shouting and cursing the land as if it was out to get them. I always thought, *How can land be bad? It's just land.* It didn't do anything except sit there and try to be left alone. It was people who were doing things to the land, not the other way around.

When I asked Papa about it, he said some people didn't want to blame themselves, so they took it out on the land instead. Made them feel better to point their rage at something that couldn't fight back.

"Like the lamb?" I asked him.

"No," he said, looking troubled. "That's something different."

The lamb was still fresh on my mind, from the Sunday before. I didn't think I would ever forget the way it squealed and screamed, with four men holding it down so the Reverend could slit its throat.

I could see the whites of its eyes, staring at me, wide with terror, pleading. Papa tried to cover my face, but I pulled away so I could look.

I wanted to see. Until I did, that is.

Then I wished I hadn't.

I watched as the Reverend plunged his hands into the torrent of blood arcing from the lamb's throat, then raised his blood-gloved hands toward the sky. Blood snaked down his forearms and into the sleeves of his suit.

"Glory be!" he proclaimed.

The lamb's blood poured down the altar and soaked into the dusty ground. Mama and Mrs. Henderson and the others chanted and swayed. Spit flew from their lips and misted the air as they intoned, "Glory be," over and over again in a rising swell of delirious rapture.

Papa was stone silent, his jaw set, his head slowly shaking side to side. He locked eyes with Mr. Henderson nearby for a moment. Something unsaid passed between them.

Once the lamb was dead, we made a line and waited while the Reverend made the sign of the cross on each person's forehead with a finger dipped in blood. I felt sick.

"What's that have to do with God?" I asked Papa when we got home afterward.

"Nothing," he said, taking a wet rag and gently dabbing at the mark on my forehead. "Nothing at all."

"Then why did the people let him do it?"

"'Cause they're scared, and when people are scared, they'll believe anything just to not be so scared anymore. To take things back to how they used to be."

"Are *we* scared?" I asked him.

Papa took a long time to answer. He looked over at Mama, who was on her knees in front of her small bedroom altar. Candlelight flickered on her face. Her hands were clasped tightly at her chin. Her lips moved in silent prayer. Finally, he nodded.

"Sometimes."

I took one last look at the photo of me and Charlie, then put it back on the table where I got it.

Mama was still digging through the closet looking for the new dress, mumbling, "Where the heck is the darned thing," and, "If he threw it away…" Finally, she gave up searching the closet and went to look for it in the big trunk at the end of the bed instead.

Wax from the melted candles was pooled and dried on the table's scratched-up wood. I scraped at some of the wax with my thumb, then picked up the handmade cross and turned it over in my hands. It had been crafted by one of the ladies at the Church of the Resurrection.

The tips of the cross were stained a dark reddish-brown, dipped in the blood of the sacrificial lamb. I guess that was supposed to make it holier somehow. "Consecrated," was the word the Reverend used. Papa changed it to a different word though, under his breath.

"Desecrated," was what he called it.

The Reverend preached that the road to Resurrection was traveled on our knees. He said if we prayed hard enough, then God would bless the ground, and the crops would rise from the dirt, just like Jesus did. Our old life would be restored. Everything would be as it was.

As it was, again it all shall be, I thought, remembering the line from the prayer Mama made me say every night before bed. *The fallen shall rise. The lost shall be found. The taken shall be returned. Glory be to the God of the Grain, praise to the Prince of the Fields. Amen.*

That was why Mama took to praying all the time, why she had Papa build the little altar beside the bed. She brought in a jar of dirt from the field, along with the blood-stained cross and the candles, and made her own little place of worship. The picture of me and Charlie wasn't there at the time. She must've added that after I left.

Mama prayed at that altar every morning, noon, and night, asking God to bring back the crop, to bring back the rain, to restore what we lost. To give her a sign that everything would be okay.

Papa got pretty frustrated with the whole charade. He said Mama spent all her time praying into a jar of dirt, instead of actually doing something useful.

"Don't you see?" he told her. "Things ain't going back to how they used to be. Times have changed. We need to change too, or we're gonna get left behind."

But Mama didn't want to hear any of that. She didn't want to change. She wanted things to be the way they always were. Change was the Devil's work, that's what the Reverend said. God made the world just so. And it was meant to stay that way.

Eventually, Papa got to the point where he made a ruckus outside the tent one Sunday after the Revival, in front of the Reverend.

"I don't know, Pauline," he said to Mama. "All this praying don't seem to do no good, as far as I can see. On our knees every night and twice on Sundays, and for what? We still ain't got no rain. Ain't got no crops either. We got dirt, though. Got plenty of that!" He bent down and picked up a handful of dirt, then threw it down. "Got a bumper crop of dirt. Dust too, hoo boy! You want dust? We got a special, two bushels for the price of one. We'll throw in a mud pie too, if you can spare a cup of water to mix it in. We ain't got none here, see?"

He said it like it was supposed to be funny, but it wasn't. Mama started to cry.

After he was done ranting, Papa got in his truck and sped away, leaving me and Mama behind. We had to hitch a ride home with Mrs. Henderson. She told Mama not to worry, that Mr. Henderson had lost his faith, too. She patted Mama on the knee.

"We'll just have to pray twice as hard, to make up the difference."

~

"Here it is. Ta-da!"

Mama finally found the new dress, all the way at the bottom of the clothes trunk. She pulled it out with a flourish and held it up for me to see.

Like my other dress, it was made from the leftover flour sacks we got from the Relief Office. President Roosevelt knew that poor folks like us used the sacks to make clothes, so he did what he could to make them nice. Mama had found a sack with a bloom of pink flowers, like the kind we grew in our garden before it dried out. She turned it into a cute dress with short sleeves and a small waist, and a belt that she braided from different colored lengths of twine.

It was nothing fancy, but she sewed it up extra fine. It was pretty, I thought.

Mama shook the dress out with a sharp *snap* and laid it out on the bed. Dust went swirling up in the air in little spirals, then drifted down toward the floor. The way it caught the sunbeams streaming through the windows made me think of God. Like maybe He was still around. Like we hadn't been abandoned after all.

"Hope it fits," Mama said. "Let's see."

She lifted my arms and pulled my old dress off, up and over my head. It was really dirty. Pretty torn up, too. She balled it up and threw it in the corner like it was trash. Then she slipped the new dress over my head and tied up the string in the back. She walked around me to the front, checking out the fit, tugging at the seams, brushing off the shoulders, picking off little pieces of thread and lint as she went.

While she primped and groomed me, I looked out the bedroom window at the Henderson's house next door. Their front door was wide open, with the screen door banging in the wind. *Mr. Henderson still ain't fixed that latch,* I thought to myself.

Charlie Henderson was my best friend. Always had been, since we were babies. We did everything together. Grew up together, went to school together, played stickball together, and—when the dust storms got so bad they blocked out the sun for a week at a time—we got dust-sick together. Ended up right next to each other at little old Mercy Hospital up the road in Boise City.

And now, we were coming home together too.

I thought to myself, *I hope Charlie's parents are as happy to see him as Mama is to see me.*

Mama circled her fingers around my wrists, lifted my arms, and examined my hands. First one, then the other. "Oh my, your nails!" she exclaimed. She was right. They looked terrible. They were ragged and torn, with semicircles of dirt caked underneath. "We've got to get these clean." She disappeared from the bedroom back into the kitchen. I could hear the water running as she soaked her dishrag and loaded it with washing powder.

While I waited for her to come back, I looked out the window again. I was surprised to see Mr. Henderson emerging out of their barn and heading toward the back door of their house. He was leaning into the wind, shielding his eyes against the sharp sting of the sand with one hand. In his other hand, he carried his rifle. He threw open the back door and disappeared inside.

Mama came back into the room, her dishrag dripping a trail of soap bubbles along the floor. She wiped the grime from my hands and cleaned my nails, then straightened up and took a step back. Her eyes got all teary.

"Glory be," she said. "Look at you. You look so pretty." Then she took me by the shoulders and turned me around to face the mirror, so I could see for myself.

I stared at my reflection in the dust-streaked glass. I didn't feel pretty.

The skin on my face was the color of dead leaves. It was dried and tight on my skull, and split in some places, exposing dull white bone underneath. There was a hole in my cheek where the teeth showed through, and a sunken black crater where one of my eyes used to be. I didn't have a nose. Half my lips were gone. I tried to say something, but my jaw wasn't working right. It just hung wide open, and a little bit sideways. That's how I could see that I didn't have a tongue.

As I stared at my ruined face, I could hear screams coming from the direction of the Hendersons' house, followed by gunshots. I started to get worried. *That ain't good,* I thought. *I hope Charlie's alright.*

I watched in the mirror as Mama took her wood-handled hairbrush and tried to brush through the mats in my hair. She was doing her best, but the bristles kept getting stuck. After a few tries, she gave up and put the brush down on the dresser. It had big clumps of hair in it, with ragged strips of rotten skin still attached. Undeterred, she gathered up what hair I had left on my head and started weaving it into a braid instead.

Suddenly, the floor shook under my bare feet. Heavy footsteps thudded across the front porch of our house, followed by the familiar squeak of the front door opening. A few more footsteps, inside the house now, then Papa threw open the bedroom door. He stopped dead in his tracks. His face went as gray as the Boise City Post.

Mr. Henderson entered behind him, still carrying his rifle. Red-black flecks of blood were peppered across his cheeks and neck and were splattered down the front of his white undershirt. His expression was grim.

Mama primped up the dress around my shoulders, then turned me around to face my father.

"Look who's home," she said. She smiled. Tears streamed down her face, cutting tracks through the dust on her cheeks.

Papa's breathing tapered down to nothing. He was silent. He closed his eyes and pressed the back of his hand to his lips.

Mr. Henderson chambered a round in the rifle.

With his eyes still closed, Papa reached out toward Charlie's father. Mr. Henderson handed him the rifle.

"Go," Papa said. His voice was choked, barely a whisper. Mr. Henderson made the sign of the cross, then backed out of the room, closing the door behind him.

Papa gripped the rifle in his hands, his finger rigid against the trigger guard. He swallowed hard.

"Anabel," Mama said quietly. "Say hello to your father." With a firm hand in the middle of my back, she guided me closer to him.

Papa opened his eyes. His face was pained.

I looked down at the floor, ashamed of my horrid appearance. I didn't want him to see me like this. I couldn't bear to have him looking at me. I wanted to crawl away, back into the dirt where I came from.

Papa reached down and nudged my chin up with the side of one curled finger. He took a moment to look at my face. Then he leaned the rifle in the corner by the door frame and dropped to one knee. He extended his arms and enfolded me in a warm hug. I hugged him back. The stubble from his cheek was rough against my skin.

I heard Mama exhale a shuddery sigh. She knelt down and embraced me from behind. We held each other like that for a while, nobody saying anything.

Finally, Mama lifted her head and looked over to the small table where my picture was. She drew in a breath, then touched Papa's arm.

"Dale," she said. She flicked her eyes toward the table.

Papa looked over. A sob hitched in his chest. In the small jar next to my photo, a bright green shoot of leaves was poking through the dirt. It wasn't like any normal shoot I had ever seen—it was twisted like a corkscrew, with a sharp tip at the end. But it was there. It was alive.

"Everything as it was," Mama said.

Papa placed a soft kiss on my forehead, then kissed Mama on the lips.

"Glory be."

THE LAMB OF STULL
BY DAVID IVEY

July 2020

Nature stands arrested, cowering at the thing cloaked behind a veil of dark woods.

Fresh silence burns in Jeremy's ears as the moon laces through a mesh of tangled branches. A foul odor, rotten like juices at the bottom of a carnival trash can, taints the air. The stench blankets his tongue.

No. No. No... The word runs in his head on an endless loop.

A shiver Jeremy hasn't felt for eighteen years crawls up his legs and through his gut, clenching around his heart with confirmation. Gooseflesh breaks out like the pebbled rind of an orange.

Death is here.

It inches closer, seeping from beyond the lawn's manicured edge.

"Please, God. Help me." Jeremy whispers the prayer—a

reflex from simpler days—knowing full well that God doesn't listen to him anymore.

God has forgotten Jeremy.

Movement. In the shadows beyond the tree line. He can just make out the wet jewels of yellow eyes. The thing's gaze sears deep—far beneath the pit of any childhood fear.

Jeremy's unlit cigarette slips from between shaking fingers and falls to the patio. The eyes bore into him and his entire body shudders. "N-n-no," he says, teeth chattering.

Had he really read those words aloud? Had he actually walked down those stairs?

No. Stop it. That was all a dream. This is, too. A nightmare. That never happened. It never—

"Jeh-reh-mee," the thing speaks. A deep, guttural taunt with strange hissing undertones. "It's time to finish what we started, Jeh-reh-mee." His name drips slow and drawn out; every syllable extended.

Jeremy's mind heaves.

A chunk breaks off the crumbling landmass of his psyche, drifting into darkness. The remaining portion comprehends only madness—true, uncaring madness. It's the same feeling that had been present when he stepped foot on that first stair. It's dogged him, waiting for the cracks so it could slip back inside, undetected. "This. Th-th-this is my n-n-nightmare," he says, fighting to regain a measure of composure.

A grunt echoes from the blackness.

"I barely remember. I-I was only twelve! Now g-go away. I'm going to wake up—"

"Twelve years old, Jeh-reh-mee? Yes. We remember... A child." Another grunt. "Children don't understand the nature of their temptations." It speaks with mock concern. "They don't comprehend the manacles holding them liable.

To children, the Devil is simply an idea conjured by adults, scaring them into obedience."

The thing sighs, inciting a long, permeating silence.

Jeremy breaks the quiet, breathing in panicked huffs. Helpless. His thoughts spiral. *How could I have been so stupid? I could have buried this curse years ago—instead of the people I loved. I could have—*

"The Devil is real, Jeh-reh-mee." The voice booms so loudly, Jeremy screams. He's barely cognizant of the warm urine spreading through the crotch of his jeans.

"I-I didn't kn-know." His voice is weak and whimpering.

"No?" It hisses. The eyes seem to smile.

Jeremy lurches back with a shout as some unseen force brushes the exposed skin of his wrist. Burning pain lances up his arm, and the air grows so heavy his ears pop under the pressure.

"You invited me. Didn't you, Jeh-reh-mee?" It grunts again, louder than before.

Jeremy's heart sprints, kicking at his ribcage. He doesn't want to answer, but the word escapes with a sob. "Y-yes."

He falls to his knees and cries out, straining his voice. "Go away. G-g-g-get the *fuck* away!"

And with a startling quickness, the yellow orbs blink out. Two hot coals extinguish in the dark. The chilled air thins as if someone opened the door to a padded ice box. A world of warmth washes in—talkative crickets, sweet honeysuckle scents, and all the goings on of a normal Kansas night resume.

Sticky with sweat, Jeremy tries to catch his breath. He can taste the bitter remnants of fear—a hint of bile swimming through thick saliva, coating the inside of his cheeks. He spits, collapses onto the concrete, and picks up his cigarette. The lighter sparks under his thumb in quick succession, finally igniting behind a cupped, quivering hand.

"Shit," Jeremy mutters, inhaling a deep drag. "Shit. Shit."

Memories of Stull struggle to form. Jumbled details surface with all the clarity of vague, watery images from the bottom of a pool.

He wipes the perspiration off his forehead and draws in another breath of smoke. *What the hell's happening?*

Jeremy taps the ash off his cigarette's tip and stands— muscles limp as wet dish rags. He turns toward the sliding patio door and his reflection in the glass looks back. A darker, less pronounced copy, mimicking his every movement.

"Am I already in Hell?" he asks the mirrored image and catches a glimpse of his wrist. He looks down to study it in the redeemed moonlight. Three lines like claw marks gouged into his skin, reddened and inflamed.

Jeremy's seen these marks before.

Three.

Another more recent memory leaps from some dark cubby in his mind as profoundly as recalling where he had put his car keys. Jeremy slowly waves a hand to his image in the glass.

"Reflection," he whispers.

Something Ellie once said poured into a subconscious reservoir for this precise moment. She had called it *The Theory of Holy Reflection...* or something like that.

Everything is bound by rules. The good and bad alike. All designed with a balance, or... What was it?

Everything has a counterpart?

"That's it!" he confirms, looking skyward.

Jeremy drops his cigarette and puts out the ember with a

grind of his heel. Somehow, he knows what needs to happen.

An answer to his prayer?

Has God remembered me, after all?

He massages the scratches on his wrist, pacing—brainstorming a plan.

Telling her will be the hard part.

"But she's the only one who'll believe me."

He nods to himself and begins to weep.

If he's right, Jeremy only has two more days to convince Dr. Ellie Mathews to take his life.

"IF WE'RE gonna do this, you can't fight me," says Ellie, rolling a small vial between her thumb and forefinger.

She stands, leaning on the edge of her mahogany desk, adorned with crucifixes and other religious relics. "Lie down, be still, and close your eyes."

Jeremy fidgets, shifting his weight on the chaise lounge. "I didn't come here for a psych evaluation, El. I came here—"

"No. You came here to ask me to commit murder, Jeremy. That alone requires a little psychiatric attention, don't you think? Can you just admit I'm right and cooperate before I decide to have you committed?"

"You're not a psychiatrist, damn it. You're a demonolo—"

"I'm trained in methods that parallel and delve deeper than traditional psychiatric practices. Listen, the spiritual realm is not far from the physical in many ways, and it's in the subconscious mind where these worlds most often collide. Trust me. It's not healthy to repress these things."

She takes a seat next to her friend and twists open the clear vial of oil and water. "May I?"

Jeremy nods.

It won't do you any good, a voice in his head insists.

Ellie speaks in Latin as she dabs the blessed vial on her finger and traces the shape of a cross on Jeremy's forehead. She repeats the ceremony for herself—a spiritual barrier of protection. "I'm *not* going to kill you." She chuckles, then furrows her brow—a look of concern he's grown to know over the years. "That's not the answer. I *can* help you, though. Your mind's refusal to deal with what happened is coming back to haunt you. The only way to move on is to face your demons. Quite literally, in your case."

She can't help you, the voice jeers.

Jeremy purses his lips and stifles a weightless argument. "Fine. But I came to you because you... Stull changed your life too, and you know it."

"Yes. I was there, but I didn't see what you saw." Ellie stands and pulls a small bag of incense from her coat pocket. She holds it above her head, uttering a prayer under her breath. "Amen."

"Amen," Jeremy echoes.

Amen. Amen. Amen. The pestering voice mocks like a child.

Ellie places the bag in a bowl stationed at the foot of the largest wooden cross on her desk, then lights the sweet-smelling offering. The aroma fills the small room. "Like I was saying, my own experience in the cemetery was, admittedly, enough to jumpstart my faith and my profession. But I've seen a lot since then, and I can tell you that sacrifice— the kind you're talking about, anyway—is not the answer here. I believe you. But there are ways to fight this that don't involve... Well... Just lie down." She walks around to sit behind her desk and reaches to turn a knob on the wall. The lights dim.

Jeremy closes his eyes. A feeling he can't quite identify, like steel wool on his nerves, creeps in with a tacky warmth.

The voice. *You can try and try and try, but all your loved ones will still die.*

Go away! Jeremy tries to focus. "I'm ready, El."

"Good," Ellie continues. "Now, concentrate on my voice and do as I say. Take a deep breath in. Hold it in your lungs for three, two, one. Now, do it again. Hold it... Let it out. And again... Now exhale. Keep that pattern as you listen to my voice. I'm going to count backward from ten. With each number you will feel yourself getting heavier as if a lead balloon is pulling you down; sinking deeper and deeper. After I say 'one,' you will find yourself on the night of March 20th, 2002. Do you understand?"

"Yes."

See you soon, Jeh-reh-mee.

"Good. If I feel that we need to end this session, I will say the word 'exit,' and you will wake up feeling safe and comfortable right here with me. Do you understand?"

"Yes."

Oh, Jeh-reh-mee. If those words you hadn't said, would your brother still be dead?

Ellie clears her throat. "Very good. Now keep breathing. Remember, Jeremy. You are here with me. This is a safe place... Okay. Ten... Think about the people you were with. Me, Gil, your brother. Nine... Your eyelids will get heavier as you imagine your twelve-year-old self. Drift back. Eight... You're returning in your mind. Let go. Seven... The sights and smells of that night are coming into focus. Six... Heavier. Deeper. Five..."

Jeremy can sense the moisture soaking into his jeans from the cemetery grass.

"Four..."

The moon highlights white headstones hugging the contour of the hill like bright floating rafts on a frozen sea.

"Three..."

A scent perfumes the air—something stale and unnameable.

"Two..."

Someone's laughter... *Jonathan?*

"One..."

He's suddenly awash in the chill of a late March evening. A gust of wind tears past, and Jeremy is twelve years old again. His mind entangles with memories, played out in tangible reality.

"Stop it," a younger Ellie pleaded with Jeremy's older brother Jonathan. "You're scaring them."

"No, it's true," Jonathan continued, ignoring her. "The occult, or Satanists or whatever, actually opened the portal to Hell back in the '70s. One of the seven portals that exist on Earth. The Pope won't even fly over this area. Stairs to the gateway are hidden, but they extend below the basement of this church." He pointed to the roofless stonewalled structure a few yards away.

"Bullshit," said Jeremy's friend, Gil. "If all that's true, then we wouldn't be here. No way you'd drive out here if you believed that."

Ellie smiled and put her arm around Jonathan. "Of course, it's not true. He's just trying to scare you guys." She kissed him on the mouth. "So, stop trying to look cool for me in front of your kid brother. You've got nothing to prove."

"Get a room," Gil said.

"We just might." Jonathan smiled. "You guys'll be fine if

we leave, won't you? Especially since there's nothing to be scared of. Right?"

"Whatever," Jeremy said. "I'd rather hang out with Satan himself than watch all this sexual tension. It's sick."

"Suit yourself." Jonathan grabbed Ellie's arm. "Hear that, babe? These two assholes wanna be left alone. I won't come running to help when good ol' Beelzebub starts dragging you guys through the gates to Hell." His eyes widened in an attempt to look spooky as he pulled Ellie back toward the Jeep parked off the road's shoulder.

She turned with a parting pout as they jogged away, hand in hand, disappearing into the shadows.

"Why did they bring us here?" Gil asked. "This is stupid."

"Dad wouldn't let Jonathan be alone with that girl. Anyway, what else were you gonna do? Play Mario Kart?"

"Whatever."

"You're not scared, are you?" Jeremy asked with a wry grin.

"No, dickhead. Are you?"

Another breeze rushed by, causing the hairs to quill on Jeremy's arms.

Hell yes, I'm scared, he thought but didn't let on. "Nah. I'm good." He clicked on his flashlight. "Let's look around."

The beam bounced off frowning facades of limestone monuments, making shadows dance through the grave-yard as they walked toward the dilapidated church on the hill.

"I gotta take a piss," Gil said as they reached the crest. He unzipped and peed against the wall.

Jeremy left his friend behind and strolled up to what remained of the church entrance. Hinges, rusted and bent, bolted uselessly to small chunks of a rotting oak door. The two stone steps in front were long cracked and crumbled by years of surrendered maintenance.

Jeremy high-stepped through the doorway into silence that somehow pulsated in his head. Even his footsteps fell muted and dull. An odor of rotted wood and mold lingered from the remnants of decaying roof lying in shambles on the cobbled floor.

Feels alive in here, he thought with a strange instinct that something about the place could hear him. See him. A stone belly of some malevolent, sentient beast. Icy air bit at him like a million little ants feasting on his skin.

I don't like this.

He clamped the flashlight under his chin, cupped both hands against his mouth, and breathed warmth on his numbing fingertips.

The beam of light caught a red image on the floor.

"Gil," he shouted. "Hey man, get in here!"

Gil's footfalls shuffled over loose stones as he stumbled through the entry.

"Take a look at this." Jeremy pointed to a spray-painted pentagram and an array of melted candles in the center of the room. Someone had pushed aside the chunks of pews, making enough space for whatever conjuring had occurred.

"That's messed up. It feels weird as hell in here."

"Nice choice of words." *He's right, though.*

"So... you think there's any truth to the shit your brother was telling us?"

"Seriously doubt it," Jeremy said, shining the light through glassless windows. *I hope not.*

"Yeah. Me too." Gil gulped audibly.

Jeremy traced the base of the far wall with the beam of light as the two boys stood shoulder to shoulder beside the ceremonial floor art.

"What's that?" Gil asked, pointing to a pile of stones near the back right corner of the church.

They looked at each other and shrugged. Without speaking, both boys crept over to investigate.

A formation of stones from a crumbled section of debris stood, stacked neatly in the form of a small pyramid, four or five rocks high in the center. Something brown stained the sides and drizzled to the floor.

"That's blood, man," Gil said. "I'm not comfortable—"

"Looks more like someone took a shit all over it to me. Something's definitely covered up, though."

Jeremy began moving the stones aside.

"What are you doing?" Gil let out a sharp whisper.

"Help me."

"We should really go, man, I—"

"Pussy," Jeremy said. The adrenaline of discovery outmatched his fear as he heaved a rock against his chest and tossed it aside with perfect shot-put form.

"I'll hold the light. I just..."

"It's cool, man. You prolly couldn't move one anyway." Jeremy laughed.

Gil flicked his middle finger at his friend.

Wooden planks began to show themselves beneath the rocks.

"Holy shit. Jeremy moved faster, tossing and scraping the remaining pieces of pyramid away. A wooden door—three marks scraped across the center plank—had taken shape. "Oh my God," Jeremy said, his eyes widening—heart pumping. "Help me open it!"

"No way."

"Come on. This is awesome!"

"We found a freaking door. Cool. Now it's getting late. Let's just go."

Jeremy tuned Gil out and tugged on a thick rope handle. The door opened as if it had been oiled daily for years. He fell to the ground, exerting more effort than necessary, and the wood door slammed open.

Jeremy stood and snatched the light from Gil, shining it into the black abyss looming in front of them.

Stairs.

The boys looked at each other—a nervous tension growing in the air.

"That's the freaking stairway to Hell," whispered Gil.

"Nah," Jeremy replied, but his breaths labored, and a sour metallic taste smacked in his mouth.

"I'm getting out of here."

"Dude, it's just stairs. Look. You can see the bottom." He pointed the light to where the stairway landed on a dirt floor about fifteen steps below. "I'll give you fifty bucks if you go in."

"I'm good. I'll give you a *hundred* dollars if we can just leave... like, now."

"You don't have it."

"Wanna bet? I'll show you. At home."

The ant bite sensation on Jeremy's skin returned. He closed his eyes and clenched his fists. *It's not even real.* "I'm gonna do it," he blurted out. "You can be witness, and we can—"

"I just offered you a hundred—"

"I want to say I did it, okay? It's not even a lot of steps. I'll go down and come right back up."

"Fine." Gil threw his hands in the air.

Jeremy lifted his foot and slowly stepped down. The first stair creaked beneath his weight, and he held his breath as ice rattled through his body. He looked at Gil, smiling. "I'm okay."

One step at a time.

Another step.

Another.

Another.

Another. His head dipped below ground level. The surrounding walls seemed to vibrate around him.

This is stupid.

Another step. The flashlight dimmed.

Another.

Another. The light blinked out with a clink.

A high note of dread sang through Jeremy's veins. A mocking aria sending a shiver through his bones.

This shit isn't real. What am I so afraid of?

Jeremy hit the side of his flashlight with his palm to cut it back on. The batteries rattled, but it remained off. He turned to look behind him, expecting to see Gil, but only darkness hovered above. He stared desperately, transfixed by the pitch-like black.

Did he shut the door?!

His breath gritted in his chest.

Are things moving in here?

Sly shiftings in the dark—menacing suggestions of activity—all attended by a silky sound that made him think of sightless spiders shucking over one another.

Don't go down any more stairs, shrilled the voice in Jeremy's head. *This is a tomb, and I'm inside of it... alone.*

A whisper from below.

Not alone.

Jeremy wanted to call out, but his voice couldn't breach the terror. His blood seized dry. Nerveless dust like fast-dry cement caked his veins.

There it was again. Unmistakable. From deeper down the stairwell...

A child's whisper.

"Hello?" Jeremey croaked. He clapped a hand over his mouth, not believing his own voice had escaped into the void.

What if someone answers?

A scratching sound came from behind him. Jeremy spun on his heel. Again—a staccato scurrying. His eyes hunted desperately.

Rhythmic panting traveled through the dark as a shape carved itself out of the gloom, just a few feet in front of him.

Dull yellow eyes.

Jeremy's throat burned with a scream he couldn't release.

"Read," ordered the whisper.

The flashlight clicked on suddenly, and Jeremy dropped it to the ground, shaking with quaking fear.

It had fallen on a dirt floor.

Did I reach the bottom already?

As he picked up the light, Jeremy swung it around, pointing up the way he had come. The stairs above him climbed endlessly, far beyond the throw of his beam.

Impossible.

"Read," the voice whispered again, and Jeremy turned with a start. His light fell on a portion of sandstone wall with small writing carved into the side.

"Read."

Jeremy couldn't fight the pressing urge to obey. Something about the voice calmed him amid the hellish terror infiltrating his every pore. He focused on the words, and with a trembling voice, managed, "Filius a tenebris. Per portam oriri. Habita intus animae mea."

A soft, insidious gargle-of-a-groan responded—low and warbling.

Bypassing eardrums, it crept into Jeremy's bones and through to his core. It grew louder with such quick intensity that dirt and pebbles shuffled and popped on the ground like water on hot grease. Not just loose dirt, but the depths of the earth seemed to join in, shifting below his feet, throwing any semblance of remaining sanity into chaos.

Jeremy couldn't speak.

Couldn't scream.

Couldn't move.

"Ex—"

Below the vibrations of moaning, a softer voice breaks through. Distant and watery, with an ever-so-slight hint of urgency. Jeremy's mind struggles to focus. Is he frozen in the throes of some incredible evil or... somewhere else?

"Ex—"

A prodding insistence from another time.

"Exit!"

~

A CRUCIFIX JUTS out of the drywall near the window as if someone had stabbed it directly through.

Ellie paces, stepping over papers, books, and other crosses strewn about the floor of her office. A smell like burnt hair floats in the room. She bites her thumbnail and mutters to herself. "I know. Twenty and three. Not twelve. No. He must be the one... Yes. I saw it, and I know..."

Jeremy sits up on the couch, muddled and confused. A burning pain sears on his forehead, and he taps at it with a finger, pulling his hand back with a sharp hiss.

"What the hell happened, El?"

She doesn't look at him as she continues repeating her soft, restless mumbling.

"Ellie, look at me. What's going on?"

"I-I saw it," she says, turning her face toward him, expressionless—a telltale sign of shock. A trickle of blood runs from her left eye. The reddened, bubbled skin on her forehead makes out the shape of a small cross.

"Holy shit! What happened? What's—?"

"Eighteen years. I-I should have realized the significance. I didn't understand what, I mean *who* we were dealing with."

"What did you see? Can you just start with what happened in this room?!"

"Jeremy." Her eyes meet his, and the first hint of sanity softens her face. "I saw... It was *you* back then."

"What does that mean?"

"Well, I know it wasn't *you*, per se. But I saw Gil. You just laughed when he smashed into the rubble. And when Jonathan..." She pauses. Tears gather and bead in her eyes. "I saw Jonathan go to help him, and you—I mean, *it*... With just a wave of your hand, the wall caved in on them both. Your eyes, Jeremy. Your eyes were so—"

"Horseshit. I was still in the stairwell when the cops came. They basically had to dig me out, El. The damn earth shook or something. *That's* what killed them. I know it was... *supernatural* or whatever, but you saw wrong. Why have you never told me this before?"

"You spoke German."

"Wha—?"

"Yes." She begins to cry in soft whimpers, the tears from her left eye mixing with the drying blood on her face. "And French, Russian, Italian. Jeremy, you spoke Latin and ancient Hebrew. And other languages I didn't even recognize!"

"Whoa. Okay, I think we need to get you some help.

You're hurt and may be in shock." A film of sweat coats his skin—saltwater stinging the throbbing burns on his wrist and forehead.

Soft whistling sounds in his head like someone calling a dog with a treat, *Hello, Jeh-reh-mee...*

Ellie sniffles and saws under her nose with her forefinger. "Under hypnosis, you talked to me. As soon as you opened the door on the floor of the old church in your memory, your eyes opened and you looked at me. Jeremy... I-it wasn't you. Not your voice. N-not your eyes." She begins to cry again.

The hairs on Jeremy's arms and neck stand at attention on sprouting gooseflesh. "What did I say?"

You know the words, Jeh-reh-mee. Come now.

"It translates loosely to..." She clears her throat and takes a breath to compose herself. "...'Son of Darkness. Rise through the gate. Dwell within my soul.'"

Jeremy flinches. "*That's* what I was saying to you?"

She nods. "Over and over and over in multiple languages. And then your back arched. You... y-y-y-you *growled* at me. You actually *growled* like an animal. Th-the crucifix flew straight past my face. My books flew off the shelves. My skin burned. I'm so, so sorry, Jeremy." Her whimpering graduates to full-out weeping that overflows into a fit of writhing in her chest and shoulders as she fights to find her breath.

"Shh. Shh. It's okay. I'm here now. I'm here."

So am I, Jeh-reh-mee. So. Am. I.

Jeremy thumps a palm to his forehead. *Please just shut up!*

"Ellie. Come on, now. There's got to be something we can do."

Oh, there is nothing you can do to break the hold I have on you. A singsong tune in his head.

"There is." She wipes her eyes and inhales—her breath stuttering to find its rhythm. "But not here. And not until tomorrow night."

~

"Are the handcuffs really necessary?" Jeremy asks, one arm chained to a steel pipe as he sits at a small table in Ellie's basement.

"I'm not sure yet, but I'd rather not find out. It's the third day since it made contact, and I'd like to be as cautious as possible."

"I get it."

She tosses a book onto the table.

"You were right about the *Holy Reflection* idea, by the way. I don't know how it came to you at that moment. I'm not one to discount miracles, but it's quite astounding that your mind brought you to a conclusion you don't even understand. God looks out for us in our time of need, I guess." She smiles. "At least I know you've read my book."

She thumbs through the pages of her one and only published work, "*To Him That Hath Understanding: A Guide to the Demonic Realm.*" "I want to talk to you about numbers so you understand what it is we're up against."

"I was never very good at math."

She frowns. "This is no joke. That night in the cemetery, I saw something—"

"Yeah. About that. You basically said you saw me murder my friend and brother. That's not—"

"That was simply a vision I had during your hypnosis. I know for certain it wasn't actually you. What I *do* remember seeing, though, I've never been able to tell anyone... until now."

Ooh, I bet this will be good, Jeh-reh-mee.

He closes his eyes, willing the voice to stay away.

"We were down at the Jeep—Jonathan and me. We heard Gil screaming, and Jonathan ran over to help. He made me stay back, but I could still see. The moon was so bright that night. Gil was... He was levitating."

"Levitating?"

"Yes. I know how it sounds, but Gil was floating over a pile of rubble by the old church walls. I couldn't move." She takes a sip of water and closes her eyes to better recall the moment. "He screamed out for help. When Jonathan got closer, Gil's body dropped—" Ellie opens her eyes and takes in a breath through her nose. "—No. Not dropped. *Slammed* down onto the stones. I heard his bones crack."

"Dear God."

"Jonathan ran over to see what had happened, and I saw three... I don't know what to call them... three *figures* appear around his body. They were just shadows—dark entities linked like they were holding hands. A dark Trinity of sorts. But one of them stared right at me. The eyes. My God, those eyes. They were a dull—"

"Yellow," Jeremy interrupts.

"Yes." She looks at him, her own eyes as blue as a glacier lake. "They were the same eyes that looked at me last night... Yours." She turns away and stands to pace the floor. "Now. Numbers..." Ellie clears her throat.

"Wait a sec. Can we talk about the whole *eyes* thing? That's—"

Ellie holds up a finger to shush him. "It was the full moon of the Equinox. That's the *third* phase of the moon during the *third* month of the year. That's *six*. You were twelve years old … *six* plus *six*. Do you follow?"

"Not in the slightest."

She can count, Jeh-reh-mee. Impressive.

He ignores the voice. "Go on."

"All creatures are bound by a numeric *Code of Three*. The Bible is chock full of it, and… Listen. March 20th. The *third* month of the year. The twentieth day. Twenty divided by *three* is six point six six. And then there's the year!"

"2002?"

"Yes. That number in multiples of *three* is admittedly 667.333. But it's commonly believed that the incorporation of Anno Domini was miscalculated by eighteen months." She paces quicker, hands animated, talking fast. "Meaning the birth of Christ occurred nearly two years later than originally thought. That suggests the night in Stull actually took place in the more accurate Year of Our Lord, 2000. If you divide *that* number by *three*, you—"

"Ellie, you have to slow down…"

"The number you would get is 666.666. It's *perfect*. Do you even *know* what time the walls crushed down onto Jonathan?"

He shakes his head. "I'm guessing it's divisible by three?"

"I looked at my phone when I called the police. It was 12:06. *Six plus six plus six. The Code of Three.* It waited eighteen years to process and contemplate the plan. *Eighteen*, Jeremy!"

Jeremy shrugs and sighs.

"*Six* plus *six* plus *six*! Look…" Ellie points to the open page of the book, displaying a verse from Revelation:

"'And that no man might buy or sell, save he that had the mark, or the name of the beast, or the number of his name. Here is wisdom. Let him that hath understanding count the number of the beast: for it is the number of a man; and his number is 666.'"

"That's... weird. But we already know we're dealing with demonic shit. What do the numbers mean?"

You know, Jeh-reh-mee.

She closes her eyes and tilts her head toward the ceiling. "Okay. So, God sent Christ to Earth. Right? Jesus knew he would die. The *willing* Sacrificial Lamb of God."

"I went to Sunday School."

"Just listen. So, he died. *Three* nails. *Three* days he was buried before the sacrifice was complete. The sacrificial transaction was bound by the *Code of Three.*"

Jeremy stares at her, eyes wide.

"Our *Theory of Holy Reflection* is nearly complete! For God the Father, there is Lucifer. For God the Son, there is the son of Satan himself... And then there's God the Holy Spirit." That look of concern again. "Christ left the person of his spirit here so that God could do work on Earth through his people." She sits back down and grabs Jeremy's free hand. "I'm so sorry, but it's you, Jeremy. *You* were chosen."

"Chosen? Who chose me? For what?"

"Apollyon... Abaddon. Th-the son of Lucifer. You are the embodiment of his spirit. You are the third reflection."

Wait for the payoff, Jeh-reh-mee.

The handcuff burns into his wrist as the tension mounts. "I didn't even know Satan had a damn son. What am I supposed to do with this information?"

"You were chosen to be the—I know it sounds crazy, but you are..." She pouts and puts a hand to her cheek. "Well, there's no other way to say it."

"Just tell me."

"You're the Antichrist."

Somewhere from the corner of the room is a deep chortle as the demon laughs in the shadows.

"This coffee tastes like shit," Jeremy says, blindfolded in the passenger seat of Ellie's car.

"Sorry. I was in a hurry. But finish it. We'll both need the caffeine. It's already late and we have a long night ahead of us."

"Come on, El. Can you tell me *anything?* I mean, where are we even going?"

"Soon. I've been praying and God answered me. He made it clear that the less you know, the less *it* knows. That's better for both of us."

"Any word from the Big Man on when I can take off this blindfold?"

"Yes. We're almost there."

The car's blinker ticks as Ellie slows to a near stop. The engine purrs forward again. Another turn over crunching gravel, and the brakes squeak. She puts it in park and cuts the engine.

"You can take it off now but understand that this was the *only* way."

Jeremy peels the blindfold from his eyes and blinks to let them adjust to his surroundings.

They sit, parked in a wing of darkness, between two streetlights, just off an unpaved road.

"Holy shit, Ellie, we're not where I think—"

"I'm sorry. It's the only way. We have to do this right, or everything falls apart. For Christ, it was Golgotha. For us, it's a different hill."

"I just didn't expect I'd ever come anywhere near this place again."

Welcome home, Jeh-reh-mee. A grunt.

They step out into a gusty night, and Ellie begins crossing the road, over to the chain-link fence that marks the boundary of the graveyard.

No cars.

No people.

The trees are only shapes, moving against a cloudy sky, backlit by a pinkish glow of the blood moon. Streetlamps dot away in perfect white circles, casting spotlights on the embankment, and adding an extra layer of security that didn't exist eighteen years ago.

"Hey, El," Jeremy says, jogging to catch up with her, "Listen, I already figured out that I have to... Well, I have to die, right? No secret there, and I've really come to terms with it. Beats giving in to this thing's plan to take over my body... Jesus, I can't believe I just said that out loud."

Ellie stops, turns around with a smile, and puts a hand on his arm. "Sacrifice *is* the most direct way, yes." She pulls her hand back and grasps the crucifix hanging around her neck. "It's just not really a possible solution."

"I'm listening."

Me too, Jeh-reh-mee. Me too.

Ellie turns again and strides forward. They walk along the fence past the gate marked, NO TRESPASSING, as moving shadows dance and twine on the roadway.

She continues, "If we chose this option—death, I mean —we'd have to acknowledge that you're already synced with a very powerful being. It's doubtful that it would allow any kind of sacrificial ceremony to take place. In other words, it would protect itself. Let's say, for argument's sake, I succeed in killing you. I stab you in the back in some unexpected manner, or slit your throat from behind—"

"Geez, El. You've given this a lot of thought."

Jeremy groans. *My damn stomach is killing me. Nerves, no doubt.*

"Sorry to be so graphic. But if I succeeded, our issue would then be the three-minute window after your death. The *Code of Three*. Apollyon has that timeframe of influence."

"Meaning?"

"Meaning it could manipulate me. It could cause me to read the inscription and simply jump into me. Not its first choice, but—"

"You know, I've been thinking. Tonight might not be the night. We could be wrong about this."

"I'm not wrong," she whispers back.

"Hear me out." He stops walking and coughs fitfully, leaning over to catch his breath. "Sorry. I'm not feeling so well. What I was saying is that it's July 5th." Jeremy coughs again. "Well, July is the seventh month. That's like, God's number, right? And it's the fifth day... Not divisible by three. All that has to mean something too, doesn't it?"

She stops and turns back, waiting for him to catch up. "It *does* mean something. I'll give you a moment to figure it out."

He coughs again, then shakes his head.

"Not to mention that tonight marks our hemisphere's twentieth lunar eclipse in the last eighteen years, but what's seven plus five?"

"Oh. Shit," he whispers.

She pouts, turns, and continues walking. "We're almost there."

They arrive at the far side of the cemetery and turn left

along the fence line. The area is shadowed by an enormous pine, surrounded by a mishmash of decorative brush.

"This is it," Ellie says, all business. "Give me a boost?" She reaches over the fence's edge and drops the flashlight to the grass on the other side.

Jeremy squats down, his intertwined fingers creating a foothold.

She steps on, grasps the top of the fence, and hoists herself over. "Okay. Your turn."

Jeremy moans again and bends over in pain. "I-I'm just nervous as hell, I guess. The stress. I-I just need a minute." He sits and leans his back against the chain-link, making it jingle against the vertical pole.

"I'm sorry, but we have to hurry. Your body's already reacting to Apollyon's advances. We only have about ten minutes to get up there and do this if it's going to work."

Oh, it's not going to work, Jeh-reh-mee.

Not listening to you.

He raises his head and takes in a deep breath, interrupted by another series of coughs. "Okay."

Willing himself to move, Jeremy finds the strength to stand and heaves chest-first over the fence's edge. He swings his legs across the top and lowers down to stand beside Ellie. "Let's get this over with."

The red moon is bright enough to avoid hazardous treading through the uncut grass. Rows of stone monuments reflect back a salmon glow. The rubble at the top of the hill, a disheveled heap.

A tomb from his nearly forgotten past.

His heart squeezes in his chest. The vision brings on fear that paralyzes his steps. *Oh, God. Please, God. I don't want to do this.*

Ellie stifles a cough of her own, "We have to hurry. Let's go," she blurts, urgency in her voice.

Jeremy groans and grabs at his stomach. "Something's wrong, El. Something—"

"Keep moving. It's him." She jogs forward.

"I—" A deep, gravelly cough. Jeremy covers his mouth, pulls his hand away, and looks down.

Blood?

That doesn't look good, Jeh-reh-mee.

Ellie calls back, "We're almost out of time. Please. Hurry!"

Jeremy falls to his hands and knees, a string of blood dangling from the corner of his lips. "I—" He groans. "I can't..."

Jeremy goes dizzy. Ellie's pleas fall muted. His eyes flutter. His vision contracts. It's as if he's seeing the world from the bottom of an elevator shaft. And then...

Jeremy begins to sing.

And to the tune of Gilligan's Island?

No, not him. The *thing* within him.

"There was a shrew who thought she knew a way that she could win. But she ran out of time and now her plan is running thin... Hello, Ehh-lee." It coughs and grunts loudly. "Let's play a game together. How about I count to *three*?" Its laughter resonates, bouncing off gravestones. The thing inside Jeremy coughs again and stumbles as it begins to hike through the linear rows of stone.

What's happening? Jeremy's thoughts are a whirlwind. *Oh, no. No. No. No.*

Jeremy can see her ahead, scrambling through the old rubble.

Stay away from her!

No response.

It labors closer to the debris and coughs again, hacking up a chunk of bloody mucus. "Ehh-lee. Yoo-hoo."

It steps over a mound to find her crawling frantically across the floor, scraping at the loose dirt.

Is she looking for the door?

"Ohh, Ehh-lee." It stops, coughs, and sits hunched over on a larger piece of rock. "I think I see what you were planning, and it's wrong on so many levels. Flawed from the start. You see—" A fit of coughing contorts Jeremy's body over. He spits out another bloody chunk. "You see, though the coffee was a nice touch, poisoning our buddy here does no good. First, it's not *your* sacrifice to give. If he doesn't *know* he's going to die, then it's not *his* choice."

Oh, El. What have you done?

Ellie cries, crawling... searching.

Please, leave her alone, Jeremy pleads from within.

It ignores him.

"Second, there's the fact that you can put as much baby oil or crosses on yourself and burn those fucking smelly herbs all day and night, but you can't ward me off, you pretentious bitch."

"Apollyon, you may not use my body—"

It laughs deeply, sounding unlike anything Jeremy's vocal cords had ever manufactured. "So, let's get this over with, my dear. We've got a lot to look forward to together."

"In Jesus' name—"

"Do *not* use that name with me!" It lurches forward and grabs her by the back of her neck. With a strength from outside Jeremy's physical body, it lifts Ellie, bringing her nose to nose with itself.

Jeremy can see the fear in Ellie's eyes.

"I believe you've been looking for this." It waves a hand, and a wooden door slams open onto the ground.

Ellie fights and screams as it wastes no time, dragging her into the stairwell with one hand.

Jeremy can sense the immense pressure being squeezed onto Ellie's neck. He can hear her cries and her feet shuffling on the stairs as they try to tear her away from its grip. Darkness is everywhere.

"Read," it whispers as something yellow illuminates the small space.

Its eyes?

"I will not," she whimpers.

"Read, Eh-lee."

"No, I—"

The sound of a lion's growl forms the word again directly into her ear, "Read." It releases its grip on her neck and falls back against the stairs.

"I. Will. Not!"

The thing inside Jeremy wretches and snarls.

"Jeh-reh-mee can still feel the pain, Eh-lee." It coughs and then takes Jeremy's thumb, pressing it in the corner duct of his right eye. The eyeball makes a sucking, squishy sound in Jeremy's head as the thumb digs into the socket and plucks. The eye pops, its jelly oozing out, bloody and thick.

Ellie screams.

The thing begins scratching at Jeremy's face repeatedly, drawing deep gashes of blood across his forehead. "He's crying inside, Eh-lee. Screaming like Gil did that night. Read. The. Words."

Jeremy senses no pain, but Ellie doesn't know this.

She coughs and leans against the wall, exhausted. "Please stop."

It reaches Jeremy's hand inside his mouth and quickly tears at the flesh of his cheek, ripping it—a sound like thick, wet cardboard. The flap of skin left dangling below his jawline.

"Okay! I'll read."

No, Ellie. Don't.

"Filius a tenebris..." She clears her throat into her fist.

"Yes. Read," it says softly.

"Per portam oriri. Habita..." Ellie moans. "Intus animae mea."

Jeremy's bloodied body seizes and growls. Thunderous pops and low, vibrating hums erupt in the small space. The earth shakes and shifts. Ellie convulses.

Jeremy is suddenly himself again, and the pain floods over him like acid. "Ellie. No." A hoarse remnant of his voice barely makes a sound. He breathes, raspy and shallow, dying on the bottom stair of Hell's gate.

The thing, now in Ellie, turns to look at Jeremy and smiles, then coughs.

"She," Jeremy tries to speak. "She..."

"Yes, Jeh-reh—" It coughs again.

"She p-p-poisoned her coffee, too. Didn't sh-she?"

The thing stares at Jeremy and cocks its head. Not speaking. But not smiling either.

"If I had t-to g-g-guess," Jeremy says and spits out a drooling, bloody pool of bile, "I'd say sh-she bought herself t-time a-a-and only used a portion of wh-what she gave me. My g-guess would be a *third* of the d-d-dose?" He chokes on a bubbly laugh and bares his teeth—his best effort at a smile.

It looks back at him, unblinking, shifting erratically like it might explode beneath increasing pressure. Strange noises hum and screech. Wailing and bellowing from somewhere below.

The noises slowly fade as Jeremy's body continues to shut down. His breathing, faint and less frequent.

And... Something else.

Another voice? Yes.

A faint whispering. "Well done, my child. I never forgot you."

A tear drips from his remaining eye and Jeremy stutters in one final breath.

The last thing he sees before everything fades away is fear.

Not Ellie's this time.

Just fear and confusion swimming in dull, yellow eyes.

NAILS

BY R.A. BUSBY

The second time Mark saw the purple fingernail, it sat beside the teachers' snack machine.

School had been out at least an hour, and the other chess club kids had scurried home, but Mark lingered, trying to be strategic about spending his dollar twenty-five. He'd pushed aside the construction-paper flyer on the front of the machine advertising "Halloween Dance '86!" with some irritation, wanting to see the candy choices still available this late in the day.

The cheapest selections slumped in Loser's Row at the bottom, and Mark passed those by without a glance. The Grandma's Cookies or Sour Patch, the ones Mark thought of as the popular kids of the concession world, sat strategically at eye level, and in the next rack down were the Fire Stix and Lemonheads. As a vending machine connoisseur, Mark believed the Fire Stix deserved a more exalted place in the hierarchy, but no one was asking him.

Gonna be the Big Hunk, he decided, but before he pressed the button, Mark glanced beyond the small alcove in which the machines sat to make sure Kenny and the eighth-grade footballers weren't around—or if they were, that he had time to stow the candy in his puffy vest before they started in on him. *Hurr, hurr, lookit the Big Hunk eatin' a Big Hunk! Git 'em, guys!*

During his year as an undergrown sixth-grader, Mark had flown beneath their radar, content with the occasional shove or six as they buffaloed down the hall to PE or the gym, for those abuses were impersonal, anonymous. Over the past year and a half, however, he'd grown taller, more substantial, and they'd noticed. If Mark had joined the football team, perhaps he could have been a defensive lineman, some moving wall of meat between the opposing team and the goal, and then his size would have been fine. An asset, even. But he hadn't, and it wasn't.

The school remained still. Mark noticed how loud the silence seemed, as if sound and life drained out when students left, and only the droning fluorescent buzz of the lights remained to tell the tale. He knew the dictionary had a word for that, the forlorn quality of an empty place normally bustling with people, but he could not recall what it was.

With a decisive gesture, Mark pressed his thumb on the button marked C-4 and heard the quarters drop into the change box. He monitored the slow progress of the machine as it urged the candy forward and frowned, anticipating the possibility that the bar would flub up its exit from the chute and hang there, a sugary Sword of Damocles. This time, though, the candy dropped into the receptacle at the bottom with an unceremonious *ponk*.

Mark felt the thing the moment he shoved open the metal slot-guard. As he reached in for the candy, his fingers passed over a hard and cylindrical shape, and at first, he thought he'd grabbed hold of a little ice cream spoon. When he drew it out and opened his hand, the object fell between his sneakers, hit the linoleum with a small but decisive *tik*, flipped over, and stayed there.

It was a fingernail. To be precise, it was one of a set of press-on nails painted the pinkish-violet shade of his mother's hibiscus.

Cutelle, Mark thought as his heart began to race. As his breath came in jagged little pants, he flashed on the memory of the bright bottle on his mother's dressing room table. *Cutelle Nail Polish.*

And just before his bladder gave way, darkening his jeans with a stinging trail of piss, Mark saw the fingernail pointing straight at him.

HE RAN down through the alley behind the school, dodging late-autumn tree branches and scurrying down streets of smug bungalows with bow windows stuck out in front like beer bellies. Mark hurried, ignoring the rasping chafe of cold denim against his thighs and holding his vest so it dangled over his crotch, obscuring everything, or so he hoped.

At Home Avenue, he nearly turned left from old habit, but that route led to a dead house, a dead life. When he reached his grandmother's, he darted around the side and came in by the kitchen, the closest entrance to the basement with the washing machine. If Gramma asked, Mark would explain he'd fallen in a puddle and was now taking responsibility for his mistakes. *Well,* he considered, *it's kinda true.*

He tiptoed downstairs and reached for the pull cord to turn on the light. The laundry room, concrete floor stippled with ancient water stains and powdered soap, lay off the larger storage area, a shadowed rabbit warren of discarded furniture and dead people's dead things. Along the far wall hung an old curtain made from the same pattern of yellow-brown roses covering his grandmother's couch. Down in the dark, the basement smelled moist, rich with the earthy tang of mold and moist bricks. Like the school, the deserted room was silent.

But it was a different silence.

Mark yanked open the dryer and prayed for good luck in the pants-or-sweats department, but the machine sat empty, laundry folded in a patient pile of his grandmother's slips, nightdresses, and (to his horror) a large beige bra with cups big as his head. On the clothes bar, though, three drooping hangers dangled, and on one hung an ancient bathrobe that had belonged to Grandpa Pete. Mark supposed it would have to do, and he shoved his jeans down, wincing as they clung to his damp and reddened legs.

He pushed aside the Borax and found the detergent, not knowing exactly what to do with it. His brows furrowing in concentration, Mark measured the detergent as if taking a lab test in Mr. Stott's class and spent a good minute reading the instructions on the washer lid. When he supposed he'd gotten it right, he poured in the soap and hoped for the best. The water hissed out over the jeans, and since he stood there already, Mark added his shirt, underwear, and socks, remembering to grab the Big Hunk still stuffed inside his pocket before it was too late.

So stupid, he chided himself, listening to the machine. *Goddamn baby pee-pants.* He frowned, pushing back the dark hair from his forehead. Above him, the house maintained its quietude, the floorboards above the old boxes and disused furniture mute and unmoving.

At that moment, Mark noticed the silence peculiar to the

basement. The school's silence had been loud, the walls and floors holding their breath for the inevitable onslaught of chattering students, knowing this stillness to be abnormal and impermanent. But this sound felt palpably different. The basement lay unperturbed by the silence, content that no one ever—

clack

came down here except to do laundry or—

tik

fiddle with the furnace.

At the sound, Mark's brows drew together. He glanced at the machine but only caught the agitator's soft *slursh* as it stirred clothes. The noise had not come from the stairs to the basement, as one might expect, but from the cold area in the corner with its makeshift upholstery curtain. The crawl space.

Crawl space. He'd never liked that term. Peering into the greater darkness beyond the laundry room, Mark imagined pushing its curtain aside to reveal a dank passage at waist level, nearly wide enough for his shoulders. The floor would have packed earth, he knew, and overhead, the beams would press down from above, spiderwebbed wood bowed with weight.

The crawl space. Where things crawl. Down his neck, perhaps, the caress of an antenna thin as thread, a long leg tapping with curious courtesy on his wrist. A tentative tentacle. A dark handshake. He shuddered.

He had stared inside it once, after all the things had happened and they had loaded her boxes from the old

No, no, no...

He didn't want to think about it. So he didn't.

With a shiver, Mark gathered the old terrycloth lapels around him, noting the fabric bore a trace of his grandfather's aftershave. Bay Rum, perhaps, or Old Spice. *Dead ten years and we still smell Pop-Pop down here*, Mark thought, wondering if the odor had just gotten stronger. At first, the scent had been faint, spicy, a cedar chest with a lifted lid, but now it had taken on an intimate, fleshier note, like the damp earth tang of the crawl space laundry room floor.

It would be tight in there. Real tight. And so... silent.

He turned to the washer. The clothes spun around in their soap bath, pausing a moment between cycles, and he supposed he could leave the machine to work its magic, as long as he might—

tik

Mark whirled around. The crawl space lay at the far end next to a bookcase crammed with water-damaged paperbacks—his grandfather's Robert Ludlum collection—and that side fell in shadow. The curtain, Mark noticed, looked askew, pulled a bit to the left. Had there been a gap before? He didn't recall.

The sound came again. At the curtain's edge, Mark thought he perceived some slight movement, a trick of light. He told himself this. Still, something appeared to have *(crawled)* fallen out.

From the opening dangled a dark hank, some object fibrous and tangled as a horsetail. A scent of fleshy flowers and dirt filled his nose, his mouth, and he could stand it no more. Mark pelted for the stairs, slamming the door behind him when he'd reached the safe confines of the kitchen.

~

HE'D BEEN TOO LOUD.

"Mark? That you?" The voice, querulous and tinny, held a note of fear.

Beside the sink, Mark froze, robe half clutched about his broad middle and puddled around his ankles as if he were one of the Seven Dwarves. *Jesus, if she comes to the kitchen, what the hell are you going to say? "Hey, Gramma, I was downstairs and thought I'd put on Pop-Pop's bathrobe now that he's dead. No reason. Normal people do it all the time."*

"Hey, Gramma," he yelled back, forcing a cheerful note into his voice, but his throat wrenched it into a dry squeak.

"Mark?" his grandmother called again from the bathroom. He had the barest chance. If he made it down the hall before she came out, he could duck into his room and change. And then what? *Stuff the bathrobe into the laundry bag. Go downstairs to put your jeans in the dryer for tomorrow. You'll need them. They're the only ones that fit.*

"It's me, Gramma," he called, more authoritatively. "I just banged the door coming in. Sorry about that." He stepped close enough to the bathroom to pick up the irregular shuffling from her old-lady slippers on the slick tile. With a dash, Mark made it to the safety of his room and closed the door.

As she came into the hall, his grandmother called, "You 'bout scared me to death with your noise. Supposed it might be Norman Bates trying to catch me in the bathroom." She paused outside Mark's door and waited. "What are you doing in there?"

For a wild moment, a laugh rose, wanting to become a scream. He bit down on his lip until the wild sound receded, and he could trust himself to speak.

"Nothing," he answered. By then, he had struggled out from his grandfather's bathrobe. On his closet floor, he found his old sweats and, breathing hard, he stuffed his sticky legs into them and opened the door.

His grandmother fumbled in her breast pocket for a

cigarette, sticking it into the corner of her mouth with professional ease and peering at him through a rising cloud. "Want one?" she asked, holding out the pack. "Teach you how to blow smoke rings."

Mark blinked, trying to think what to say. "I'm in seventh grade," he answered at last.

Gramma snorted. "Aren't you fancy? I picked up the habit when I was ten." Winking at him, she blew a twisting O of gray smoke which undulated in the afternoon sunlight.

He stared at his grandmother in her old pink t-shirt, her arms speckled like a rainbow trout. Owlish lenses made her eyes into twin-poached eggs, and her hair fell in an unkempt halo shot through with the red hair she'd passed on to his father. Mark tried to imagine his grandmother as a girl, from the Little Rascals era perhaps, but found it impossible. She had always been old. She'd emerged from the womb already wrinkled, a cigarette in one hand. Mark could only say, "I read somewhere those give you cancer."

She snorted again and waved a dismissive hand. "We all die of something, boy." Gramma's eyes met his, and neither spoke for a minute. "I made tuna casserole," she said, patting his shoulder. "The kind with the egg noodles from the Jewel. Takes about a half hour in the oven. You hungry?"

To his surprise, Mark found he was.

THEY ATE in the TV room. He hated the TV room.

In the center sat the old couch with its yellow-brown roses the same as on the basement curtain, flowers like the ones throughout the house last year with their heads bowed down. Not long after the boxes were stowed away in the crawl space and Mark moved in with his grandma, he realized the couch sat in an especially frigid corner, as if a chill rose through the very floorboards from a cold, unmoving thing that lay below.

Mark and his grandmother sat shoulder to shoulder, tuna casserole plates balanced on twin TV trays. Gramma preferred to heap the evening newspapers on the far cushion, leaving Mark to fish in the pile for the schedule.

"You looking for this?" His grandmother tossed a TV Guide into his lap where a sultry blonde stared up at him from a cover with the headline, "How Hollywood Almost Crushed Kim Novak." He flipped through the magazine with a sigh, knowing Gramma would turn to some show such as *Highway to Heaven,* and Mark would be pinned between her unyielding hip and the old paper pile, right above the cold spot.

Mark thought of Kim Novak being crushed.

"You feeling okay?" his grandmother asked, elbowing his ribs. "Your face looks longer'n Bill Buckner's when he flubbed the grounder Saturday like a fool. You don't want it?" She pointed with her fork at his casserole.

"I'm all right." Mark turned toward the TV, not seeing it. "It's great, Gramma. Honest."

"You ate this the first night you ever ran away from home, remember?" His grandmother gave a laugh that turned into half a sigh. "You with your pillowcase all filled with your stuffed animals and a few Star Wars books. Damn miracle you got here in one piece, little bitty thing that you were." Gramma sat back on the couch and clicked through the channels.

Mark ran the string of his sweats through his fingers but did not reply.

"I fed you some casserole, called your house, and ten minutes later, your mother comes clackity-clackin' up the front stairs with those high heels of hers, black hair swinging, and we went to it hammer and tongs. Spitting out the old poison that was building since your daddy passed, I suppose. Hoo boy, didn't she have a temper?" His grandma ruffled his hair. "You've got her coloring, but the rest is all my Jackie." She pointed at the picture on the mantel.

"I have to fold my laundry," Mark said after a long pause. He eased to the edge of the couch, shifting the TV tray away.

His grandmother handed her plate up to him with a shaky hand and lit a cigarette. "Anyway, you recall what I told you? I promised you could stay here any old time. And here you are. You remember, don't you, Mark?"

And because she smiled then, and because her eyes behind the wide spectacles shone in the light, Mark nodded and took the hand she reached out to him in comfort, feeling an infinite sadness at its dryness, the fragility of an old woman's wrinkled fingertips, and thought he could recall nothing from that night but his mother's cold silence on the cold drive home and for nine cold days thereafter.

"So," Gramma said to him in the morning. "What do you want to do for her?"

Mark blinked down at his plate of eggs and English muffin. An amber bead of butter hung suspended on the rim. "Sorry?"

His grandmother snorted. "Boy, do you think I came into this world ass-backward? You know what I mean. I'm not fooled by your fooling." The smoke from her cigarette lazed and drifted in the kitchen air, weaving in and out of the dust motes. "It'll be a year come Friday, so you've got yourself a day to cogitate about it."

When Mark said nothing, his grandmother sighed and lit another cigarette. "Do a kind of remembrance," she said. "Light a candle. Go to the grave. Maybe go through those basement boxes with her stuff and figure out what to keep and what to leave. Do something." When he did not reply, she added, "You know, it's good to feed the dead."

The bite Mark had taken felt too large for his mouth just then, and he swallowed hard. "What do you mean 'feed' them?"

Surrounded by the gray halo of smoke, her hair lit by the sun, his grandmother resembled an ancient witch, if ancient witches wore t-shirts with pictures of Starsky and Hutch.

"They eat memory." Gramma nodded. "My gran told me that, and I'm telling you."

"They eat—?"

"You heard me." She got up and poured herself another coffee. "I know the feeling," Gramma said, sitting back at the table. "It's hard to face the dead, so you want to put 'em behind you. Lock them out. Stick their shit in a box. Stick *them* in a box. Stick it all in a box down in the dark underground. You think *Out of sight, out of mind*, and hope if you stop remembering them, they'll fade away and let you be. That about right?" Her eyes went sharp behind her glasses, and she tapped a finger on his wrist to emphasize her words. "But that's not how it works."

Mark poked at the rubbery edge of his egg. The orange juice he'd had earlier curdled in his stomach as if he'd swallowed lye.

"They eat memory," Gramma repeated. "When you stop remembering them, they starve."

The words burst out from him in a rush. "Good," Mark

spat. "So starve." Eyes wide, he clamped his lips together in a thin pale line so he could say no more.

His grandmother's fingers circled his wrist. "You don't suppose I know how that feels?" Her voice hardened. "Trust me, I do. But Mark, when you starve the dead... they get stronger. Angrier." She nodded at the wall calendar. "'Specially now."

He didn't know what to say. Looking out the window for the school bus, Mark got up from the table and slid the eggs into the trash can uneaten.

HE COULD ALWAYS COUNT on Mr. Martinez to let him go to the bathroom during pre-algebra, but today, Mrs. White was his substitute and wouldn't let Mark out until almost too late. Now, he bowed over the toilet, a humble supplicant with hands on his trembling knees, wondering if the sour volcano in his stomach would give it up and gush it out already.

By some miracle, the bathroom had been empty, and Mark had chosen his favorite stall at the far end, the one hardest for creeps to peek into. Usually it was also the cleanest, but not today. Along the inner rim, someone had left a dark brown spray that made his guts roil. *Ass chocolate*, Mark thought as his stomach gave a hitch. With a loud *yark*, he heaved a stream of half-chewed egg and acid juice from breakfast.

With a shuddering breath, he wiped his mouth and poked at the toilet paper dispenser, the kind designed to give out one parsimonious sheet at a time. Using his ballpoint, Mark scraped out a sad handful and did his best to clean up after himself, unlike the previous occupant. "Sorry," Mark whispered to the silent bathroom, eyeing the floor ruefully. At least he'd gotten most of it in the bowl. Most.

Dizzy and weak, he sat down on the toilet and leaned his cheek against the cool tile wall. With some amusement, he noted the requisite dick drawn on the stall door facing him, and beside it a penciled question, "When did I eat CORN?" On the other wall, some bathroom artist had drawn the Stussy "S" seventeen times, each one perfect, architectural. He wondered if the Stussy fan drew one whenever he took a crap, and supposed he probably did.

He closed his eyes, relishing the absolute silence. Beyond the walls, students chattered, teachers lectured, but here, in this corner stall, the world kept quiet, and he could catch his breath before he had to—

click

Mark's eyes flew open. *Mrs. White?* For a horrid second, he imagined his math teacher standing at the boys' bathroom door, beehive hair swirled up like gray cotton candy, knees concealed by her humorless hem, her feet planted in a square-toed pair of old lady shoes.

"I'm coming," he called, his voice too high. "Sorry."

Only silence answered back.

But... there's someone there, he realized. *I can feel it.* The quiet, which had been so peaceful before, took on a hushed, expectant quality, as if the air had thickened, and he caught a sound slight as a plastic spoon tapping on the tile.

tik

Puzzled, he glanced down at the floor of the stall next to his. He'd known it had been unoccupied because the door hung wide open, but now there seemed to be... a presence.

Mark stood, fingers gripping the little metal latch. *Lift it, chickenshit. Lift it and head back to—*

tik tikittytik TIK

—your math class.

There came a shuffling *click*, and again Mark thought of a woman's shoe. Then a slow almost luxurious *scriiitch*.

Five purple nails now lay beneath the dividing wall.

Pointing at him.

You yes you did it

The silence grew louder. His breaths came in spasmodic gulps that did not fill his lungs, and in his terror, Mark shoved himself against the door and tried to raise the latch. It would not open. His throat closed to the width of a cocktail straw and he heard himself make a series of little whistling sounds as he breathed. Mark glanced down again.

Now there were seven.

As he watched, they raised and lowered themselves one by one, tapping on the blue and white tiles of the floor. The sound felt deliberate, punctuated.

tik

tik

tik

tik

tik

tik

tikkitytik

They did it again. Then faster.

The purple nails scraped along the tile in jittery, skittering movements Mark could not quite follow because to do so would drive him insane. Panicking and lurching, a mindless wild thing, he shoved against the door, wheezing with the effort. The nails tapped faster, came closer, and in that instant, his mind threw up a memory of a silent woman in a silent car, fingers drumming on the hard plastic of a steering wheel while she waited for the light to change.

tik tik tik

Mark looked down again.

Now he saw nine. And they were tapping so very, very fast.

He turned to the lock and tried to work it. As he moved aside, Mark sensed something pulling him, a tickling, delicate thread encircling the naked skin where his socks ended.

He saw black strands of hair spidering out toward him in a rush, fanned out like the ends of old rope. He jerked his ankle away, his foot hitting the wall, and only then did he realize his weight had been forcing the latch against the plate, making it impossible to lift.

With a half scream, he raised the latch and stumbled out into the bathroom, half falling, not knowing what he would see when he passed the open door. He ran and did not look behind him.

MARK RETURNED to math with a few minutes to spare, earning himself a lecture from Mrs. White, but that was all right. The longer he stayed after school, the less likely he'd be to run into Kenny. Again.

As Mark had rounded the corner from the bathroom on his way back to math, he'd smacked into him, and in that instant knew a vicious glee when the older boy rocked backward on his heels and slammed with a clang into the seventh-grade lockers.

"What the FUCK, McAllister, you asshole!" he yelled. Mark risked a quick running glance over his shoulder and saw Kenny break into a run for a few steps until Mrs. Simic stepped into the corridor and asked Kenny how much he wanted a referral. Mark didn't catch Kenny's reply, but overheard Mrs. Simic tell Kenny he could have two for the money: one for class disruption with vulgarity, and the other for insubordination to a faculty member.

And although he realized this would be a bill he'd have to pay, and soon, Mark walked home with the lightest heart he'd had in more than a year.

"WELL?

Mark had waited to leave until he was certain Kenny wasn't lying in ambush. He worried his grandmother would be angry that he was late, but she bellowed a "Hello" from the bathroom as usual. He'd dawdled over changing from his school clothes while she waited in the TV room, and when he came in, she patted the sofa cushions for him to sit. On the TV, a soap went to commercial. *Guiding Light*, he guessed, but they all looked the same to him. She turned the sound down.

"You decide to do anything yet?"

Mark kicked at a tuft in the old shag carpet. "About what?"

"About what? Good Lord, I guess I must seem a dumbass to you." She snorted, tapping her cigarette pack on her wrist and teasing one out.

"No, Gramma." Mark relented. "I don't—I don't want to do anything for a memorial. I realize I should, but I just don't." He blinked, hating the prickle of tears. His fists dug into his belly to make its sudden twisting stop.

Her hand quivering a bit as it hovered over the TV tray, his grandma handed him a water glass. "Take a sip," she said, cocking her chin.

"I'm not thirsty."

"Didn't think you were. I said take a sip. It's an old trick: if you drink water, you'll wash away your tears. I did it at your granddad's eulogy. Had that bottle of fancy-schmancy Evian up there with me, and every time those tears choked my throat, I'd drown them with the water." She gave a short barking laugh. "Probably everyone thought it was gin."

He drank and found the tightness in his throat eased. "I'm sorry, Gramma." Mark stared down at his feet. "I guess I'll—I'll do what you want."

She snorted again and tapped his knee. "Aw, hell, Mark. I'm not gonna force you to do jack shit. I've told you what's what, and now it's for you to decide. Not me. Folks grow in their own time, like flowers. Can't make one bloom before it's ready or you'll mess it up something awful. Bottom line," she said, "it's your choice."

The glance he shot her was hot and suspicious, but he saw no flared nostrils, no narrowed lids, no grim half smiles. He only saw his grandmother's face, broad and plain, eyes wide behind the enormous lenses. He ducked his head and took another sip before trying to talk. "Are you going to be— I mean, you won't be mad? You'll still..." He took a third sip. "You won't stop talking to me?"

She stubbed out the cigarette with a decisive tap in the old amber ashtray and tilted her head, her brow furrowed. Her hand came up to his chin and she lifted it, looking in his eyes.

"You kidding? Of course I won't stop talking to you. Why the hell would I do something like that?" And at the note of genuine puzzlement in her voice and her soft hand on his face, Mark let himself cry at last, not minding that his grandma rocked him against her shoulder like a child until the tears were out and done.

ON FRIDAY, he opened his locker.

The nail was there. It pointed at him from the cover of his math book.

Mark slammed the locker door, but not before making some half-strangled squawk that attracted attention up and down the 400 corridor. His cheeks reddened, and he wished he could call it back. He opened his locker again and reached inside, trying to grab his book without looking.

"What a bitch," hissed a voice into his ear, the breath hot and smelling of Cheetos. Mark didn't have to turn around to know who it was. "What kinda sound was that, McAllister?" Kenny inquired with mock concern. "Your baby balls get twisted in your panties?"

Mark shot a quick glance to where Mr. Pietrowski, the hall monitor, stood leaning against the upper stair rail, his back to them. There would be no help from Pietrowski anyway, he knew. The guy's monitor motto appeared to be: *Let the kids fight it out amongst themselves.*

Oh, fuck this, thought Mark, and with that, the events of last week—of last year, to be honest—landed with a sandbag's weight on his shoulders, and he felt weary beyond words. *That's it, already. I'm done.* He gave a mental sigh and turned around.

"No, Kenny," he replied, loud enough for his voice to carry. "It's the sound your mom makes when she's dancing on my big ol' dick. Yours is way too small, she says."

There was a silence, then a cataclysmic explosion of whooping laughter. Kenny's head snapped from one side to the other in quick assessment, and he took a step forward. Mark might have beaten a quick retreat before Kenny beat him first, but the locker door pushed into his shoulders and forced him forward.

Instead, he straightened to his full height and dared to look Kenny in the face. *Is this the first time I've ever truly seen him?* Mark could not recall. The other boy's tiny blue eyes narrowed in rage, his fair freckled skin all blotched and furious. But Kenny, Mark noticed, was looking *up* at him. And then he looked away.

Holy shit, thought Mark. *I think I won.*

"I'll find you later, McAllister, you fucking asshole," Kenny hissed.

Mark nodded and gave a cheerful one-finger wave. "Hey, lift up your mom's bedcovers whenever you want, Kenny. I'll be there."

The hall burst into more whoops and hollers, enough to draw Pietrowski's momentary attention, but the bell started ringing anyway. Mark reached into his locker and saw his algebra book, the nail still pointing at him. With a grimace of disgust, Mark grabbed the text, shaking the nail onto the linoleum tile without touching it. *Fuck you, too*, he thought. *Fuck you, too.*

HE STOOD before the candy machine, and in the suspended afterschool silence, Mark felt an odd sense of redoubling.

Again, he stared at the selections, giving Loser's Row a cursory glance and noticing nothing new. Only the Big Hunks had been bought up, which was typical for a Thursday. The Grandma's Cookies remained, and the snack vendor, apparently in a witty mood, had stuck them next to a bag of Mother's. *All you need is a Sugar Daddy and a Baby Ruth, and you could have the whole candy family,*

Mark thought, amused. He hesitated between the two, eventually choosing Grandma's, and watched with familiar apprehension as the cookies dropped into the bottom receptacle.

He bent down, then paused, remembering. The nail. Swallowing, Mark shoved open the little door, half-expecting to feel a cylindrical plastic curve on top of the cookie wrapper. *Hey! Maybe when your hand is all the way in, it'll come and seize your wrist and won't let go! And when you struggle, the machine'll fall over on you, and you'll be crushed like Hollywood crushed Kim Novak!*

But this didn't happen. He reached in and grabbed his cookies, that was all.

In the deserted hallway, the wrapper's crinkle sounded outrageously loud. He'd grown to hate silence, its oppressive stillness, the way it made thoughts echo and rebound, voices in an empty auditorium. *If I save forty bucks, I can buy a Walkman down at Radio Shack,* he thought. *Maybe even the sports kind.* He imagined himself jogging through the dappled green light in the forest preserve, music playing through his earphones and all silence banished. *Flock of Seagulls, perhaps. Or Tangerine Dream.* He liked the idea. Liked it a lot.

And then, for the first time in a year, he allowed himself to remember his mother.

She'd loved silence. Been a master of it, really. It had been everywhere. Mark remembered the silent house, the silent rooms, the way silence sneaked into corners and hid behind doors, silence so loud not even MTV or cheery chirpings from veejay Martha Quinn could banish it, silence enforced by the tight, angry press of her lips into a razor-thin line, the swinging arc of her black hair as she stalked with heel-heavy steps from room to room, and above all, her silent seething fury at something he had done or hadn't done.

She never spanked him, or at least she hadn't ever since he'd gotten older. *No,* he corrected himself. *Not older. Bigger. There's a difference.*

Yes. There was, wasn't there? But she could always wear him down with invisible pressure from her silence, day after silent day, until his spirit broke and he would come to her, weeping, apologetic, no longer sure what he had done, not anymore, but sure, by God, he had done it, and ready to say anything, anything to crack the silence lying like the groaning frozen surface of a midwinter pond. And he would catch the quick upward flicker of her lips, the shadow of a triumphant little smirk.

And then one day, Mark had enough. He'd woken up one morning and known. Without a word, he stuffed his backpack with his clothes, schoolwork, mixtapes, books, and broke the two weeks' silence between them to tell her he was moving in with Gramma.

His mother did not turn, but sat unmoving at the breakfast table, nails tapping in irritation on her glass. "Be there at school when I pick you up," she'd ordered in return, but he resisted this obvious attempt to bait him, closing the door quietly as he left.

And after school, he *had* waited, after all. He remembered that: the waiting. Obediently, slave to habit and hope, he'd waited in his usual spot at the eastern entrance facing the wide median where parents made U-turns. From the porch overhangs across the street, Halloween decorations danced in the early evening breeze, and some kids had already emerged with their little plastic pumpkins in their hands for trick-or-treating, and still she had not come.

Mark had peered up the avenue but did not see her car.

*It's a trick. Not a treat, but a trick. Yeah, I get it. Joke's on me, Ma!
Make me wait for hours and then pick me up when she thinks I'll
be ready to apologize and take it all back. Or she's leaving me out
here until I walk home alone and pound on the door in the dark
for an hour before she'll let me in and, even then, she won't say
anything until I cry and cry and tell her how sorry I am and—*

tik

The sound cut off the memory like a knife. Mark
glanced around at the deserted hallway and saw nothing
but the trophy case, the door to the teachers' lunchroom,
the motivational poster on the counselor's office and then—

tiktiktiktiktiktiktiktiktiktikittytiktiktiktiktikTIK

At first, Mark did not quite understand.

It came with a jittery, tapping sound like swarming
beetles, carapaces clashing, ticking and clicking with
robotic, insectile purpose as they advanced in a swarm,
closing the distance between them.

The nails.

The purple nails were everywhere.

As he watched, his mind not processing the sight, tens of
thousands of nails crawled toward him in a vast sideways
wave along both walls, clawing and tearing through notices
on the bulletin board, the flyers for the ACT, Mrs. Steiner's
poster of Michael J. Fox. The nails flowed over the floor in a
rippling purple carpet, clicking and clacking over the old,
streaked linoleum the janitors had swept that afternoon.

The fluorescent hall lights dimmed as the purple mass
passed over them like a nest of cockroaches each with its
own pinpoint purpose and drive. In the silence, he could
almost hear their thoughts, their group intelligence and it
was a kind of buzzing and ecstatic murmur.

tiktiktiktiktikTIKTIKTIKTIK

And as the mass of squirming nails advanced down the

hall, pouring over doors and into lockers, Mark saw something heave and undulate beneath them, black and flowing like hair.

His mind sent up a troubled thought. *Hey, Mark! You wanna go?* His feet refused to move. *How 'bout it, Mark? Make like a tree and leave? Make like a banana and split? Make like the Exorcist and get the hell out?* Still, he remained there, his eyes fixed on the dark web of hair weaving across the top of the hallway in spiderweb filaments. As he watched, the hairs met, twisted, met again, and advanced.

It's a net, he thought. *It's making a net.*

At that, he broke and ran, pelting down the three steps to the entrance and throwing himself against the door's steel entrance bar. The sound of the clittering nails was deafening and Mark knew they were immediately behind him, but the door resisted, and Mark howled out loud in a mindless fear and certainty that they would be upon him. Then he shoved the other end, the one farthest from the hinge, and the door opened so easily he spilled out onto the concrete, inches from where he had rested and waited for his mother a year ago.

He half fell, feet tangling, and in that unbalanced second, Mark felt a deep and aching wave of need to turn and look at what he was fleeing, to lie back and accept his loss at long, long last. *Just give up. Let her win; it'll be easy, so easy, just a minute and then...*

But he caught himself with a fingertip brush against the rough cement and pushed himself up, running in awkward, stumbling terror down the short walkway to the street, half-crazed and screaming.

"Mark!" Someone plucked at his sleeve as he ran, and he yanked his arm back reflexively. The effort spun him around and into the hood of a parked car where he sprawled, his breath heaving in and out, realizing then that he had fallen across his grandmother's dusty station wagon.

His grandmother put her hand on his shoulders, eyes wide and fierce. "Jesus, Mark. What the hell—"

He straightened, not able to look behind him, and encircled his grandmother's shoulders, surprised to feel her bones so tiny and birdlike beneath her t-shirt. "Gramma, it's not safe. You've got to lock yourself inside the car because there—" Mark swallowed hard, then swallowed again. "There's something bad back there," he told her, suppressing the fear that followed. *Can it swarm us? Can it come out?* He thought it could, but he understood another thing. *It waits in silence. It waits for me because it wants to get me alone.*

His grandmother glanced over his shoulder. *She'll tell me I'm playing games. To stop being a baby. Or that I'm crazy.*

But she did not. Looking at her face, Mark realized she only saw the ordinary world behind him: the entrance to the school, the leaf-fallen trees, the glass-fronted door. He could still hear them, the nails clittering and tapping, led by some darker conscious will lurking beyond that door swung open like an inviting mouth.

comeincomeinwehaveatrickforyoutiktiktikTIKTIKTIK

"You don't see it." His voice fell flat and dull. "You don't hear it."

She shook her head. "Nope. I don't." But then she added, "I don't have to see it, Mark. I see *you*. That's enough for me. You're grayer than old cheese. It's there, all right. Anyone with eyes can tell that."

He shook his head. "Then why don't you see anything?"

"Probably," she told him, "because it's not *my* ghost. It's yours."

"Gramma, I don't know what to—"

She put a finger on his lips. "Hush, Mark. Of course you do. I told you and my gran told me, and you're a thinking boy with brains between your ears. You know exactly what to do."

And he did.

Mark turned around.

The nails filled the entrace to the hall before him, writhing around each other in a heaving, jittering mass through which the black hair wove like tentacles. They would grasp him, he knew, claw him, grasp him, draw him down the throat of that dark and wriggling bore, and perhaps that would be the last thing he would ever see or hear.

"I remember," he said to the squirming mass, and he did. "I remember you."

A year ago, Mark had waited there until the daylight dimmed, his gloved hands stuck deep into his jacket for warmth. *She wants me to come home, but she'll pretend not to hear me at the door. I'll knock and knock, and all I'll hear is silence.* He'd nodded, then, deciding things for good, and instead of heading down Home Avenue, he turned right toward his grandmother's house and stepped into the wide, deserted street.

Mark had nearly crossed to the grassy median when he saw her car approaching in the fading daylight. He paused in the road, pinned in her headlights' glare. In the dim light, he glimpsed his mother in the car, hands gripping the wheel, and for a second, he wondered if she would even bother to slow down. She pointed to the school sidewalk behind him, jabbing with one thin finger. *Get back*, the gesture ordered. *And when I stop at the crosswalk, get in the car.*

Mark almost had. He'd even made a little half turn with

his shoulders before he stopped and changed his mind. Taking off his winter glove, he lifted his hand high. Then he gave her the finger.

He ran to the median and across the other lanes in five quick steps. Soon, he would be at the runners' path that wound through forest and grass, safe from her car for the moment. Behind him, he heard the furious shriek of her brakes as she approached the U-turn, her car pivoting around the median. She would pull up beside him, he thought, and demand he go inside.

And from one step to the next, his world entirely changed.

Behind him, Mark heard a dull *thonk*.

So quick. So quick. All the sounds happened at once. A high, shrill horn. The metallic *thonk* of car on car. The bright shatter of glass. And then a silence.

Before he could think of it, his feet started moving toward the accident, and that was when he saw her.

His mother lay sprawled over her hood, head hanging cockeyed and loose. Her black hair tumbled over the edge and blew in the gentle evening wind like waving grass. Beside it, her arm dangled down, blood dripping from one white finger. The press-on nail she'd worn on it had vanished.

Two weeks later, Mark saw the nail she'd lost. It was lying in the street by the crosswalk.

Pointing at him.

"I remember that," Mark murmured, staring at the open school entrance. "I remember." The din from the clattering, tapping nails before him grew louder, became a chittering rage-howl in his head, the inarticulate bellow of white-lipped fury. "I remember you." Holding his grandmother's hand in his own, he said it again and again until it became a kind of prayer for the dead.

Each time he did, the sound diminished, and at last, only the wind remained.

He stayed there, wanting to see it done. Finally, it was.

After a while, Mark squeezed his grandmother's fingers. "We should get home, I guess." She nodded, but they stayed a bit more. "And Gramma," Mark added, "I'll—I'll clear out the stuff from the crawl space like you asked. Go through it. And afterward?" He smiled. "Maybe you can teach me to blow smoke rings."

"Naaah." His grandmother shook her head. "Some smarty-pants told me that shit gives you cancer."

The wind blew down the street, but still they did not leave. It was silent, Mark realized, but it was a good silence. In the gathering dusk, a cluster of little kids passed, herded down the sidewalk by a brace of bored fathers. There was a ninja, Mark saw, and a witch. The final girl gave him a wave. On her hand was Freddy Kreuger's glove.

"Great nails," Mark told her, waving back. "Really great."

ROOM THIRTEEN

BY JULIE HINER

Friday, February 13, 1976

The bulbous moon cast a glow over the deserted road. The chill air stung Thomas' lungs. A bag of fresh-baked sourdough dangled from his fingertips, taunting his stomach. He shuffled his red high tops along the sidewalk, watching the clouds of his breath. Grumbling erupted in the pit of his belly. His nagging mother better have dinner on.

A single caw from above shattered the silence. Pins pricked the back of his neck.

Thomas brushed a dirty blond curl away from his eye and looked around. Nothing. Could traces of that weed he'd shared with Joe behind the school still be lingering in his bloodstream? *Nah.* That was nearly six hours ago. It was an early birthday present from Joe. The big thirteen. Only three more years, and he could run from this horrid place.

He scratched at the fresh pimple that had sprouted in the middle of the birthmark on his chin. His mom's voice hounded his ears. "*Tom-Tom. You're almost a teenager. You have to choose. Greasy chips, or acne.*" He kicked at a stray pebble, hating his lot in life. Everyone in this stupid town called him Tom-Tom. The nickname had been bestowed upon him when he was two years old. It was an unfair tragedy. He'd been too young to shield himself against the childish label when it was stapled to him for all eternity. He needed to escape this shit town. He hated everything about it. Even the name. *Grimshaw.* It was grim.

He tightened his grip around the plastic bag. It was only six o'clock, yet the sky was three shades away from black and the moon was on high volume. It stared down at him with an icy glare, a tint of blue frost coating its cratered surface.

A chill trickled through Thomas. Could the moon be cold? He shrugged off the thought and picked up his pace.

What was he thinking? Whatever temperature the moon was, there was no way he could feel it down here.

Thomas rounded a corner. He froze. Goosebumps sprouted down his arms.

In the middle of the silent street, a tall, black figure loomed. Dark, feathered wings stretched out of either side of its skeletal body, white stripes lining them like sketched fingers.

Thomas' heart palpitated. He clenched his teeth and blinked hard.

The street ahead was empty. What was wrong with him? He could have sworn he saw something.

He stared into the darkness, scolding himself for being ridiculous. He continued walking, searching his brain for remnants of the winged, black silhouette.

Dammit. Joe must have lied about the potency of the joint.

As he rounded the last corner, four blocks from his home, his feet glued to the pavement. A bony man stood, half a dozen steps in front of him, staring and pointing a skeletal finger.

The wrinkled man spoke in a raspy whisper. "They shall come. For you." His thin lips curled into a sick, yellow-toothed, viscid smile, making Thomas' stomach curdle.

What the hell was this old kook talking about? Thomas glared and advanced along the sidewalk. The man stumbled into the center.

"Get out of my way, man." Thomas charged past, brushing the weirdo's shoulder with his own. The man disintegrated into dust.

Thomas stopped dead in his tracks. His brain buzzed. A chill trickled down his spine. *What the hell?*

The man was gone. Silver dust coated Thomas' shoulder. A pile of the same dust sat on the sidewalk beside his sneakers.

Double dammit. Not only did Joe smudge potency facts, he must have laced the birthday treat with something.

Thomas gripped the plastic wrapper housing the bread and lunged forward, needing to see his run-down house. Three steps into his final march, a loud hissing shattered the silence.

Thomas swallowed against the bile rising in his throat as he looked up into a pair of black, beady eyes. A long, hooked beak pecked at his head. Thomas waved wildly. The bread went flying, slices flinging through the air, scattering on the sidewalk.

Thomas' hand scraped against rough black feathers. His stomach seized. He gagged on regurgitated, acid-coated turkey sandwich. The massive beak punctured his flesh over and over, leaving his face covered in bloody holes. His scream lodged in his throat. Sweat sprouted over his neck and trickled down his back.

Thomas fell backward. His skull cracked against the pavement. Blood seeped, steaming over the cold ground. A thousand flutters united in a single colossal swoop as a swarm descended upon him. His vision blurred as dozens of sharp rostrums plunged into his eye sockets, pulverising his corneas to a pulp.

Tom-Tom wailed for his mother. He was as helpless as he had been the day the label was stuck to him. In a fleeting thought, he realized he'd never escape it now. Thomas lay in a mess of breadcrumbs, his eyeless face turned up at the frosty moon, gasping his last breaths.

Thursday, January 12, 1989

THE OPEN ROAD stretched out like a black serpent. The moon glared down from a charcoal sky, casting a hazy glow over the horizon. Billy wondered why she had left so late. Dilly-dallying, as she always did, not able to get her rusty green Pinto packed up and hit the road as planned.

A sigh slipped through her lips. Her eyes wandered over to the pile of items thrown onto the passenger seat. She rifled through them.

Her fingers latched onto the tattered Menthol package she'd snagged from the decrepit gas station in the last shit town she'd blazed through. Her pointer slid down the piece of yellowing tape that had been used to close the torn package, making it new enough to sell in a shit gas station in an equally shit town. The only package left, it had been her only choice, if she wanted to stop the constant shaking of her hands and still her nattering teeth.

A red glow flickered as the small flame from her purple lighter ignited. She tossed the lighter onto the passenger seat, glancing at the Flaming Lips logo plastered on the side. She inhaled deeply. The mint-laced tar seeped through her, stilling her hands, settling her choppers. The buzzing in her mind hushed. The road ahead steadied.

She willed her heavy eyelids to stay propped open, contemplating how far she could make it. If Bill Senior was driving, they'd be on the road all night. They'd make it to Nana before sunrise. But she wasn't Bill Senior. She was merely the junior version with a vagina. Bill Senior had made several things clear through his shift as a parent. First and foremost, she was supposed to be a boy. Second, because she was *not* the boy she was supposed to be, a natural-born weakness infested her.

Billy snorted, inhaled the last bit of minty smoke, then turned the crank on the door three times, just enough to crack the window. Cold rushed in, scratching frozen fingers across her forehead and clawing icicle nails through her long, black locks.

She popped the butt out the crack, then yanked the crank with vigour, sealing the window again. She reached toward the dash and turned a knob. Hot air blasted from cracked plastic vents. The Pinto was old, but the heater was solid.

A wail from the tiny speakers caught her attention. She turned the volume up on the radio, releasing the screeches of Axl Rose, asking Billy if she knew where she was. Oh yeah, she knew where she was. Somewhere between Bumblefuck and Nofuckinganywhere.

A glimmer from the bulging moon caught the edge of a sign on the side of the road. *Grimshaw.* She half snorted, half laughed. Not Bumblefuck. Not Nofuckinganywhere. Grimshaw. Population 666, according to the sign. How up to date was that count?

She grabbed at the crumpled heap of a road map on the passenger seat. Shaking it until it sprang open, she glanced across the bright-red line she'd drawn from her start to her finish.

She spotted Grimshaw, then searched for the next dot. Several inches of red line ran between the two. At least 100 km. Another hour and a half at the top speed the Pinto could manage. Towns were spread thin in the Canadian prairies. Clouds sifted over the moon, stealing the glow that had been her guide. Her eyelids threatened to close tight. She yawned.

Grimshaw it was, then.

She took the turn-off, then rolled down the main street. She eyeballed the dozen or so buildings. A neon sign flashed, signalling the *Mo-nlight Inn.* Billy guessed one of the O's had burned out. An orange-red glow lit the small office. Two cars and one truck occupied the parking lot. The single, long building looked ready to cave in. She kept driving.

In a flash, she was at the sign marking the end of Grimshaw. Grimshaw wasn't more than three blinks of an eye. She pulled an erratic U-turn in the middle of the deserted main street and drove back to the *Moonlight Inn.*

She pulled into a parking spot close to the glowing office, cranked the car into park, and thrust open the creaky door.

As she walked toward the office door, she pulled her fuzzy fake-rabbit-fur jacket close to her chest and hoped that no one had ever been murdered at the Moonlight Inn in the town of Grimshaw.

BILLY STARED at the red-orange glow emanating from the front office of the Moonlight Inn. The crisp night air stung her lungs, jolting life into her.

She contemplated a smoke, then trying to make it to the next town, but an image of her green Pinto flying over the side of a ditch stopped her. A neon sign buzzed, plastering blue-purple letters on the dark pavement. What the hell was this place?

Stuffy heat rushed her as she flung the door open. A claustrophobic, rectangular space flooded with bright light. The smell of stale sweat engulfed her.

No one was behind the counter. A radio, perched on a wooden stool, crackled and spat out a country song from another decade. A silver bell sat on the counter next to a handwritten sign. *Ring for Service.*

Billy hit the bell with a flattened palm. A sharp ding vibrated over the failing voice of an old cowboy.

A figure crept from a door in the far right corner. A shaky voice followed. "Be right with you."

Seriously. How does this place stay in business?

Billy tapped her fingers on the counter to the meandering beat. She looked around the room. To her left, the office opened up onto a lounge area with a small coffee table and several armchairs that badly needed re-upholstering. She wandered into the room, noting the aromas of cheap coffee and stale donuts.

Towering over her, on the back wall of the lounge, was a tall set of shelves lined with dead animals. Billy gasped, her hand rushing to her mouth as her feet planted into the thin, sticky carpet. Rows upon rows of stuffed and groomed creatures stared down at her with beady black eyes.

"I see you found my collection. Impressive, isn't it?" a raspy voice said, intruding on her shock.

She spun toward the counter. A wrinkled man stumbled, stepping forward with his right leg, pulling a limp left foot behind. *Plunk, shhh, plunk, shhh.*

Billy yanked her gaze from the lame foot and found her voice. "Uh, yeah. Impressive." *More like weird and gross.*

"They used to be my only work, my creatures. But they don't bring in enough to keep the missus living up to the standard she's accustomed to."

Billy pictured an old woman hiding behind a purple gown of silk, diamonds drenching her arms. She almost laughed out loud.

"You need a room?" The old man smiled, exposing yellow teeth, every second one missing.

"Uh, yeah." She smiled back, shifting foot to foot and not making eye contact.

"Twenty-five dollars. Cash only. Checkout time before noon."

Cash only? Billy dug through her bag and produced some wrinkled bills. She smoothed them out and handed them to the man.

He reached a mole-dotted arm across the counter, extending his bony fingers, and clutched the bills. "Say... if any of my creations caught your eye, I could give you a first-time purchaser discount."

Billy blinked. She looked back at the towering wall of dust-covered varmints. "Uh, no. Thank you." She zipped her bag closed. "You got cable?"

The man's overgrown eyebrows pointed down between

his eyes. "Not out here. But the telly's got good local coverage."

"Cool."

The man turned to the wall and scanned a board lined with keys. He clasped a keyring with his claw-like fingers and set it on the counter. "Room thirteen. Just got a makeover. It's real nice." His chapped lips broke into a grin, exposing yellow teeth and gummy gaps. "You be sure to let me know if you need anything. I don't always remember the nice touches like Mildred did." The man froze and stared. His smile disappeared.

"Mildred?"

"My wife. She used to run the place. She's... slowed down. I moved my business in here and started helping more." He waved a gnarled hand at his dead zoo. "Now she hardly comes down."

Billy shuddered. "I see." She grabbed the key and turned to leave.

"Sleep tight. Don't let the bed bugs bite."

Billy made a swift exit and beelined for her Pinto to retrieve her bag, shaking off the weird feeling clinging to her. *It's late. I'm tired. It's just a small town full of weirdos.* She would sleep, then get the hell out of here.

THE HINGES HOLDING the door to room thirteen at the Moonlight Inn looked like they might disintegrate. Billy eased it closed behind her and latched the rusty security chain, blocking out the dark night.

The aroma of old people blasted her as she meandered across the tattered, burgundy carpet. A soft red glow ebbed from a bulb beneath a velour lampshade perched on a table in the far right corner.

A TV from two decades ago sat on a dark wooden dresser chipped with tales of time. A phone, the numbers on the dial nearly rubbed off, sat beside the TV. She wished she had someone to call. Her mother had vanished so long ago, and Bill Senior had fried his liver with booze and kicked the bucket several years back. Nana was too far gone to even know Billy was on her way. She sighed and continued her scan of the low-budget room.

A bed, spread with a pink floral pattern and decorated with silky throw pillows, nestled in the left corner. She walked across the room and dropped her bag onto the bed.

Looking for more light, she turned to a night stand next to the bed. Something large and black perched on the small table.

A jolt shocked her internal system. Her feet glued to the carpet. She stared. Frozen.

The dark, skeletal frame stretched out past the edges of the nightstand, wings hovering.

Billy forced her feet to move. She edged her way toward the looming figure and pulled a small chain dangling from a lamp wedged in between the shape and the wall.

The light glowed.

The black thing lit up. Dark, thick feathers shone, smoothed over a sleek, sinewy body. Wings stretched out in either direction. White lines etched the feathers like sketched fingers. Ash claws gripped the scratched wood. A chalky beak ended in a sharp hook. A pair of glassy black eyes pierced into her.

Billy shuddered. She looked away and focused on dumping the contents out of her pleather knapsack into a pile on the bed. *Freaking taxidermist hotelkeeper.*

She rummaged through the pile, found her oversized

GnR t-shirt and a small plastic baggie housing her bedtime medicine. She changed into the t-shirt. She could feel the dead stuffed bird staring at her. She tried to pretend it wasn't there.

Billy opened a small fridge underneath the TV. A row of tiny bottles lined the door. She grabbed them all, shuffled back over to the bed and sat down. Her shoulders slouched and a pout tugged at the sides of her mouth as she wished she could get to her Nana. Her Nana's face floated in her mind, a ray of sunshine casting a warm glow over the crappy evening. She shook off the thought and lined up the bottles on the bed. Captain Morgan, Tito's, Jim Beam, and her favourite—Jose Cuervo. She opened the rum and shot it back. For a split second, the coconut aftertaste took her to a beach. She sighed, looking around the reality of the junk room.

She couldn't resist. The beady eyes pulled at her. She twisted her head and stared at the bird.

The golden glow from the lamp cast an eerie silhouette on the carpet. A dark, crudely shaped shadow with a rough body and towering wings. She looked over its body, finding its beady-eyed stare. The head was bald, the neck thick and scruffy.

What the hell is it?

It didn't look like any crow she'd ever seen. She contemplated putting it in the closet for the night. A chill trickled through her at the thought of touching it.

Billy tore her gaze away, snatched up the Jim Beam, and gulped it down. She pulled the plastic baggie open and retrieved a tightly wrapped joint.

Her buffet of weed and booze would dim out the black bird, the general weirdness of this place, and induce the sleep she needed to get back on the road. She sighed, thinking of her Nana's face, wishing she could have driven through the night. Sparks flew as she snapped the wheel on her purple Flaming Lips lighter. She breathed in deep.

The sweet lavender-laced smoke infused her. She exhaled, immediately took another drag, and tried not to think about the dead black bird towering on the nightstand.

BILLY'S EYES SNAPPED OPEN. Cold sweat drenched her t-shirt, sticking it to her shivering body. A dark figure loomed over her from the ceiling above. She bolted upright. The springs in the bed creaked. The mattress bounced underneath her. She cranked her neck back and stared up.

No fucking way.

Her stare glued to the pair of glassy eyes looking down on her. Her hand shook as she reached across and pulled the little chain dangling from the bedside lamp. A golden glow brought the dead black bird to life. As if in midflight, its skeletal wings stretched out, its sleek black body plastered in thick feathers floated above her.

Cold gripped her heart. She threw the thin bedspread away, bolted for the door, scrambled to release the security chain with her trembling fingers, and fled the room.

She ran barefoot across the icy pavement to the front office. She gasped against the cold air and her racing heart. The lights were on.

Dozens of dead eyes watched her as she ran up to the counter and pounded her palm repeatedly against the silver bell. Sharp *bings* echoed through the office, lingering even after she'd subsided her aggressive summons of the taxidermist hotelkeeper.

She crumpled against the counter, wiping away an

escaped tear before Yellow-Tooth could see it. The old man appeared from the back room. He plunked and shuffled his way over to the counter, his slimy smile making her insides curdle.

"What seems to be the problem?"

"That damn crow. It *moved*."

He stared at her curiously. His bushy eyebrows rose. "Oh, you must mean Mildred. She's not a crow. She's a Black Vulture. One of my most special creations. I found her, on the side of the main highway. Seems she got struck devouring her last meal."

Billy's brain contorted. She sputtered the only word she could muster, "What?"

He smiled. "Black Vultures love a good roadkill. Lots of that around here. They have hooked beaks, so they can have a filth-free feast on innards."

Billy swallowed against the sick churning in her stomach. "Whatever that thing is, it moved. It's dead. Stuffed. And it *moved*." What was wrong with this old cuckoo?

"Let's go have a look, shall we?" He shuffled his way around the counter and waved a gnarled hand toward the door.

It took far too long to get back to room thirteen at the clomping, scuffling pace the man was able to muster. When they finally made it, the door clung to its hinges, swaying back and forth. Billy tucked in behind the man, following him through the doorway.

"Well, she seems just fine."

Billy peeked from behind the man. The bird stood on the nightstand in the very position it was in when Billy had first entered the room.

It couldn't be. She scanned the empty ceiling.

The man shuffled over to the bed and stared down at the

pile of tiny, empty bottles. She followed his gaze as he looked over the bed, finding the joint butt squished into a cheap plastic ashtray.

"You may be weary from your travels. Perhaps your mind is a little... foggy?" He peered at her, one bushy eyebrow raised.

Heat rushed her cheeks. She stared at the bird. "I know what I saw. That damn thing was up on the ceiling, over the bed."

"No need to get hostile with Mildred. She doesn't like bad energy." He shuffled over to the nightstand, stroked the shiny black feathers plastering the skeletal frame, then turned and walked back to the door. "You best get some shut-eye, miss, if you plan to continue your journey tomorrow."

The hinges creaked as the door closed behind him. Billy stood, her feet frozen, cold sweat sticking to her skin. The radio clock over on the dresser told her it was 3:03 a.m. She stared at the black, beady eyes. The only thing that made sense was to listen to old Yellow-Tooth. She walked to the bed and plopped down in defeat.

Billy closed her eyes, forcing out the images of the dead, black bird. Taking several deep breaths, she willed herself to find sleep.

THE WHITE POPCORN ceiling glared down at her when she opened her eyes. Sunlight trickled in from the small window next to the door. Her mind raced through the images of the evening of terror in the Moonlight Inn. That damn dead bird. What the hell had the old taxidermist hotelkeeper called it? *Mildred.*

An icy wave sliced through her. Didn't he say his wife's name was Mildred?

She sat up in the bed and rubbed the crusts of sleep from the corners of her eyes. She pulled the thin, scratchy bedspread away. An array of tiny, empty bottles rolled down the bed, clinking together in a discarded pile.

She sighed. She needed to get away from this shit town. She needed to get to her Nana. Before it was too late. Why hadn't she been able to drive through the night? Maybe Bill Senior was right—she was weak.

No. Stupid thoughts. Car accidents happened when people drove tired.

She found the tattered carpet with her bare feet, glancing at the nightstand. A second ice wave cut her core. The nightstand was empty.

Mildred was gone.

What the flying fuck?

Billy frantically pulled the plethora of horrific images from her restless night in this ramshackle shithole from her mind and sifted through them. She could have sworn the old man left that damn bird on the nightstand.

Huffing, loud breaths, she stood and walked across the room. She grabbed her pleather knapsack and tossed it on the bed. As she stripped off her GnR t-shirt hardened with dried sweat, all she could think about was getting out of here. She pulled on black leggings and a fitted AC/DC t-shirt. She ran her fingers through her tangled dark hair and tied it back in a rough ponytail.

She sat on the bed and pulled on her black Doc Martens, then grabbed her knapsack and headed for the door.

Billy walked to the office, burst through the door, avoided any eye contact with the rows of dead, stuffed creatures, and dropped the key on the counter. She was thrilled old Yellow-Tooth was nowhere to be seen. She snuck out without a sound and sprinted over to her green Pinto. She slid into the driver's seat and turned the key.

Click. Click. Click.

What fresh hell?

She turned the key again.

Click. ZZZ. Click. ZZZ. Click.

No way.

She tried again. The clicking deepened. The engine was dead.

THE STEERING WHEEL smacked hard into Billy's palm as she hit it over and over. Why? Why was this happening to her? She needed to get to her Nana. Before it was too late.

Fuck. Fuck. Double fuck.

She flung open the door, slammed it behind her, and strode back to the office of the Moonlight Inn. Old Yellow-Tooth perched behind the counter, grooming Mildred. She glared at him.

He looked up, one hand resting on Mildred's back. "Thought you'd left when I found your room key on the counter."

"My damn car won't start."

"Well, I reckon I could call Burt for ya." He smiled, his gums looking gummier than last night.

"Burt?" She raised an eyebrow.

"The town mechanic."

"Swell." She rolled her eyes, leaned back against the counter, and stared at the dozens of beady eyes examining her.

"Help yourself to breakfast."

She followed the smell of grease and burnt coffee over to the lounge area. A small buffet was set up. Her stomach roiled against the bath of booze she'd given it.

She grabbed a plate and piled it with bacon, powdered eggs and burnt toast. Flumping down into a dusty chair, she glared at her breakfast companions hovering over her from the towering shelf.

The eggs disintegrated as they hit her tongue. She scanned the coffee table, finding a fresh copy of the *Grimshaw Grim* hot off the press. She took a big swig of cheap coffee to wash away the powdery egg residue and snatched up the paper. She snorted at the front-page headline, offering her a dose of sunshine on a shitty day.

"Maddox Murders Anniversary."

What the holy hell was this?

"Today marks the thirteen-year anniversary of the fateful day on which the bodies of thirteen boys, all thirteen years of age, were found scattered throughout the happy town of Grimshaw."

Sentence fragments popped out at her. *"Mac Maddox... hovering over the thirteenth boy. An out of towner... staying at the Moonlight Inn. All the boys... empty eye sockets."*

The final sentence stung her eyes. *"Maddox took his own life while in custody in the Grimshaw town jail."*

The paper snapped against the table as Billy threw it down. She needed to get out of this place. Now. Her gut told her the chances of that happening were about the same as someone coming in here and buying up all the beady-eyed, dust-covered creatures staring down at her.

A CHILL SEEPED into her bones as Billy walked down the main street of Grimshaw. She pulled her fake-rabbit-fur jacket closer around her. A brightly painted café stood out against the other faded buildings.

She welcomed the warm air as she entered the café. *Sweet Child O' Mine* blasted from a tape deck. The smile of a twenty-something guy with long golden hair lured her over to the counter. His nametag said *Wolf*. She perused the handwritten menu.

A tangy musk snatched her attention. She looked up into a pair of dark eyes. *Well, hello.*

"What can I get you?" He smiled, revealing a deep dimple.

She was a sucker for long hair and dimples. "Uh, coffee. Black."

He smiled wide. "Coming right up. Where're you from?"

"Not here."

"That's obvious. No one interesting is from around here."

Interesting. "What about you?"

He slid a cup of coffee across the counter. "Here. Sorry to disappoint you."

"I'm not disappointed." *What am I saying?* Her Nana's face flashed through her thoughts. *I don't have time for this. Or do I?* Her Pinto would not be ready today. What else was she going to do? Sit in a room with a dead bird?

"No?"

"Not at all." She opened her purse.

"Oh no. On the house."

"Thanks." Her insides tingled. "Say, what's this thirteen-year anniversary... the Maddox murders?"

He stood taller, pressing his palms into the counter. "Just

a weird thing that happened a long time ago. Town won't let it go."

"I saw the morning paper. Kind of creepy."

The dimple vanished. "Thirteen years ago today some guy murdered a bunch of kids. Wish the town would move on. They cling to this thing." A silver shimmer flashed across his dark eyes.

"How could one man kill thirteen boys in one night?"

His eyes darkened like storm clouds. "He did it. Then he blew his own brains out. Apparently, his face was unrecognizable. No one ever came looking for him."

Billy shivered. Where did that smile—and that dimple—go? "It's creepy." She took a tentative sip of coffee.

Wolf slid a lock of golden hair over his ear. "I'm sorry. It's just... my mom put the fear of God in me after it happened. I was eleven. The boys who were killed were thirteen. She said if I had been born two years earlier, I could have been dead."

She needed to change the subject. "Is your name really Wolf?"

He smiled. The dimple returned. "Yeah. My mom. She's superstitious. Wanted me to be a survivor."

"What time do you get off, Wolf? A girl, new in town, might need someone to show her around."

"Not for a few hours."

"That'll do."

BILLY LEANED FORWARD in the stiff, plastic chair, and stared at the bright screen. The microfilmed news article brought to life the grim day of Friday, February 13, 1976, in the town of Grimshaw. She stole a glance at the greasy-haired librarian perched behind the counter, nose deep in a book. He hadn't been too pleased with her interest in the town's history. She returned her attention to the screen.

The story unfolded in front of her like a slasher film. The images were rough, crude, and laid out like the portfolio of a budding horror film director, slapped together for a last-minute pitch. The writing was raw, unfiltered.

Manoeuvring the machine, zooming in and out, she worked her way over the article. Thirteen images of thirteen-year-old boys came to life. The first one was Thomas—or *Tom-Tom* as he had apparently been fondly referred to by the townsfolk. *Townsfolk. Who talked that way?* He had been the first boy found that night.

Tom-Tom's body had been discovered at midnight, only four blocks from his family's home. They'd searched for him for hours, yet no one had seen him sprawled out on the sidewalk.

Due to the plummeting temperatures in a prairie mountain town on a chill winter's night, the skin down his back had fused with the icy pavement. They'd had to pull him off, scraping thin epidermis remnants from concrete. Frozen flesh stretched over his face, capturing his final expression.

A brown birthmark scarred his chin. Scarlet holes littered his face in a gory collage. His eyes... were no longer eyes. They were black caverns.

Billy stared at the photo of Tom-Tom. Cold fingers slithered through her insides. She swallowed and continued to absorb the gruesome story.

She read and re-read the words. *Tom-Tom. Thirteen years old. Eyes gone. Skin stuck to the sidewalk. Four blocks from his house.* Why hadn't anyone seen him?

Her eyes moved over the images of the other twelve boys. Similar stories. All sent out to do errands for their mothers before dinner. All found in their own neighbour-hoods. Every single one of them had no eyes.

How could thirteen boys go missing on the same night in a tiny town and it took hours to find the mutilated bodies left out in the cold?

Where had their eyes gone?

The article described the empty caverns left in the faces of each boy as completely shelled out. As if something had scooped out the eye matter. Billy's mind jolted. What was it the old man said about the Black Vulture's beak? Shaped like a hook. Could ladle out innards without soiling feathers.

An ominous ball pulsed in the pit of Billy's gut. Ridiculous. Would a bird peck out eyes entirely? And Mac Maddox was crouching over the last kid. Suddenly, she questioned everything. Why was she here? Why did *she* need to know what happened to these boys? Why had she been stranded in this town on this night, the anniversary of such a grisly horror story?

She dug into her purse, retrieving a package of Hubba Bubba. She unwrapped and popped a bright pink square into her mouth. Biting into the sweet strawberry sponge, she chewed, producing much-needed moisture over her dry throat. Part of her wanted to walk out of here and go over to Burt's Garage. She could put some pressure on old Burt to get her Pinto working. Another part of her knew that was an impossible feat. For some reason she felt she needed to stay here, pull apart the article, and find out what happened to these boys.

She leaned in toward the screen and continued reading, trying to ignore the cold stare of the librarian from across the room.

BILLY USED her furry jacket as a shield against the frigid wind. She spotted the sign for the *Tasty Treat*, three doors up. She hoped the one bar in town served a stiff, cheap drink. She'd spent three hours holed up in the town library, absorbing the events of Friday the 13th of 1976.

Body odor fused with stale beer violated her nostrils as she pushed open the door. Her body relaxed in the rush of heat that hit her. She squinted. Her eyes adjusted, exposing a crusty layer covering the tattered carpet and wads of saliva-coated gum sticking to the tables.

Luscious locks grabbed her gaze. Wolf, leaning back against a wooden chair, smiled. His dimple appeared. Her insides tingled.

Licking her lips, she made her way across the sparsely populated room. Her day improved by a billion percent as she thought of the double tasty treat she was about to dip into. A shot of tequila, and a luscious wolf.

"How was your afternoon in our lovely town?" The dimple deepened.

Heat flushed Billy's face. "Intriguing. Quite the library you've got here."

"Library?" The smile vanished, taking the charming dimple with it.

"Yeah. I perused the newspaper archives. Thought I should read up on this weird murder anniversary if I'm gonna be here all night."

A silver glimmer flashed across Wolf's dark eyes. Cold sweat sprouted across Billy's back, despite the heavy clouds of heat clinging to the room.

"Look, I'm sorry. I couldn't help it. It's too creepy. And, I mean, that I ended up here on *this* night..." She bit her bottom lip, pleading at Wolf with her eyes.

The strange shimmer vanished from his gaze. He smiled, revealing the dimple once again. "Yeah." He shook his head, golden locks bouncing over his muscular shoulders. "It *is* creepy. I forget what it must be like for a stranger coming here and reading about what happened. It just... it still spooks me."

Billy reached her hand across the table, resting her palm on his bulging bicep. "Look, we don't have to talk about it." She smiled playfully. "How about a drink? I need some entertainment."

"I can provide you with that." His stare bored into her, shooting electricity through all her internal organs. "What's your poison?"

"You like tequila?"

"Sure." Wolf waved across the room. A petite waitress looked up from behind the bar, her long, raven hair catching a glimmer off the pot lights. "Trina, two shots of your best tequila, with beer chasers."

Trina nodded.

Wolf shifted his gaze back to Billy, finding her eyes with his, looking like he wanted to devour her. Her insides melted.

THE WALLS of the *Tasty Treat* closed in on Billy. Hot air suffocated her. She scanned the row of shot glasses lining the chipped wooden table, counting eight. Four each. She was sure they'd been sitting here for several hours.

Why was everything hazy? She'd had plenty of hard party nights, consuming way more booze than this, and even throwing in some weed or acid. Never had she experienced this. The walls creeped in toward her. A thick haze filtered everything.

She pressed her palms onto the sticky table and stood. "I... need... to go." Her tongue wouldn't cooperate.

Wolf stood, grabbed her elbow and leaned in. "You okay?" His face loomed, sprouting into six Wolf faces.

She grabbed her coat and bag and bolted for the door. Ice air hit her face. Her senses livened. She tried to run, reaching a slow trot at best. She had never wanted a junk room with a dead bird so bad.

Her lungs stung with every breath. Her jelly legs stumbled along in a clumsy jog. She could see the end of Main Street, marked by Mary's Marvels, the strange shop packed full of trinkets. The Moonlight Inn was around the corner. She could make it.

Panting snatched her attention. Turning her neck to investigate, she continued her pathetic amble.

Wolf. A block down, running for her, his hair whipping wildly. Why could she hear him? He was a block away.

"Billy," Wolf said, his voice a growl clawing at her ears.

What was happening?

Panic shot through her. Her right leg seized. She stumbled, hitting the cold pavement and skidding across the ice. Tiny shards ripped into her palms as she slid to a stop. She looked back. Wolf had gained on her. His eyes... that silver shimmer had taken over, transforming them into a demon stare.

She pushed herself up and summoned her strength. Rounding the corner, the neon sign of the Moonlight Inn pulsed. The soles of her Doc Martens fought against the slippery ice. The red-orange glow of the front office beckoned her. So close.

She flung the door open with a force she didn't know she had. Yellow-Tooth lurked behind the counter, staring back at her, exposing a gummy grin.

Mildred perched beside him, enduring a night grooming. Billy stumbled into the room. Beside the dead vulture, a photo album lay open. A boy looked up from a clipped newspaper article, a brown birthmark splattering his chin. *Tom-Tom.*

"Please... need... help," she managed.

The old man tilted his head. "Don't worry, girlie. We'll help you."

A panting-laced growl vibrated through her spine. She spun. Wolf stood, his hellhound stare boring into her. She leaned against the counter, shooting the old man a last plea with her eyes. He stood, gummy grin confirming he wasn't on her side. She swallowed as her stomach plummeted.

Her right leg gave way completely. She crumpled onto the stiff carpet.

Crawling toward the dead zoo, staring into dozens of glassy eyes, she imagined her Nana's voice, telling her how much Nana loved a good little girl.

A hand grabbed her neck. Something pierced her back. The rows of creatures spun in a strange collage of taxidermy. Blackness followed.

THE POPCORN CEILING swirled as Billy opened her eyes. Sweat trickled from her head, pouring down her cheeks. Her temples thrummed. The back of her head throbbed.

She scanned her hazy surroundings, making out the TV from two decades ago, and the empty nightstand bathed in a red glow. The walls of room thirteen sighed, pulling out, then collapsing into her.

Billy's mind buzzed, images of the last two days clicking together like puzzle pieces.

Wolf. His luxurious golden locks. His cologne-laced animal odor. His demon eyes.

Yellow-Tooth.

A plunking-shuffling noise scratched her ears. She turned her head, looking to the door. The wrinkled old man shambled toward her, his sticky grin making her sick. An ominous breath of air swirled through her.

The old man cleared his throat. "Cyclic sacrifice. It started thirteen years ago. Give up thirteen boys of the ripe age of thirteen, or a bad curse would descend upon all who lived here. People are more attached to their peaceful way o' life 'an their thirteen-'ear-old sons. Even my Mildred sacrificed our Tom-Tom. Then, she became one of them. The Black Vultures. They're people, of sorts. Can take on different shapes. Who knows how long they'll be here. Until all the fresh meat is gone, suppose."

"Mildred?" Billy squinted at the old man's wrinkled face. "She was your wife? And now…"

"She's a shape shifter."

"No. None of this can be real." Billy shook her head, her crusty hair scraping her cheeks.

Yellow-Tooth tossed a paper onto the bed next to her. The headline shot off the page.

"Friday, January 13, 1989." Yesterday.

"Slaughter in Small Town."

The pictures of thirteen boys, eyes gouged to nothing, splashed across the front page.

"Last night, an out-of-towner staying at the Moonlight Inn was found hovering over her last kill, fresh blood on her hands."

A chill shot through her.

"Billy Brighton took her own life while in custody in the Grimshaw town jail."

Dry heaves hoisted from her mouth. She hunched over, crumpling the paper in her hand, staring at the photo of herself.

The old taxidermist hotelkeeper clomp-scuffled across the room, halting at the door. "Told you we'd help ya, miss. You get credit for the cyclic sacrifice of 1989. The one that saved Grimshaw from a black curse." His slimy gums made her stomach roil.

The door clicked behind him. She bolted upright. She had to get out of here. Now.

A flutter snatched her gaze. Mildred hovered over her, wings stretched out, beady eyes boring into Billy's soul. Mildred swooped. The hooked beak bottom pierced Billy's eyeball. Tendrils of pain shot through her skull. Eye fluid mixed with blood blurred Billy's vision and trickled down the side of her face. She clawed at the massive bird, clutching rough feathers and tearing them out. Mildred screeched. Sharp claws dug into Billy, ripping her flesh. The hook dug deeper into her eye. The room flashed. Dozens of black vultures appeared and swarmed in one foul swoop.

Billy's body convulsed in wild spasms.

Razor rostrums poked holes over Billy's body and dug the eye meat from her sockets. She screamed at the swarm of vultures to stop. Every nerve ending Billy had blazed.

Panic swirled through her stomach and up her throat. She gagged. Acid-laced bile trickled from the corners of her mouth. Pain sizzled her skin.

Nana's face flashed in her mind, one last time.

THE HUMAN STORK
BY ZOLTÁN KOMOR

The wingless dead stork had been lying on the roof for more than a week now, its legs staring at the sky like some kind of bizarre lightning rods. The burning summer sunlight withered the bird into a mummy full of feathers and bones. The crows carried away its flesh. The flies laid their eggs in it and the terrible smell lured the snarling stray dogs from the village into the courtyard.

"I'll take that fucking thing off now!" the swine-herd boy growls. "I can reach it with a rake from a ladder. Then the hounds can have it."

Tears well up in his young wife's eyes at these words.

"Just let it stay for another day," she begs. "Maybe the wind will blow it down anyway. I don't want you to fall off that damn ladder."

Then she begins to rub the boy's hand softly, gently, in a circular motion, like if she was trying to wash her hands with soap, though she knows this touch will just get her more dirty, because the lad smells of pork shit as usual. But the boy is weakened by her touch. Sometimes the girl felt she could love this boy she had been married to for only a year and a half. Nothing can be buried during such a short time, at least she kept convincing herself of it. But then she stares into her husband's dumb, sparkling eyes, which remind her of wet pebbles turned from the ground, and suddenly she hears the words of her mother in her head: "That bastard is too stupid for you! You're just wasting your youth on him."

Indeed, she's never thought otherwise. The maternal voice echoing in her skull cave began to transform into her own. Yes, this boy is stupid and it's still hard to think of him as a man, even though he's nineteen. No, she never had illusions about him. If her father hadn't forced it, she wouldn't have thought of marrying him. If he was good-hearted it wouldn't be a problem if he was just dead above the ears, but she wasn't sure the boy even had a soul: for the most part he just stared blankly forward like a frog crouching on a stone, expecting nothing special from life.

"I'll take that fucking thing off now!" he will say tomorrow too, but she's going to persuade him again not to do so, since she wants a baby from the swine-herd boy. And not as the result of loving him, but precisely because she doesn't. She needs someone who she can love in this house. Without anybody to love, what else is there for her in this home? Only the cracked clay and straw walls, these cold prison bars all inhaling in silence, stealing the human breath. And the all-encompassing mud, the pigs roaring outside, the tears dried in the grains and, of course, the pee-stained toilet plank.

"If you have fucked with the boy, you must marry him!" her father ordered. She could swear she had almost never heard him curse before, so hearing those words felt like a slap to her face. But she couldn't argue with him because, yes, she had really fucked with him. Only many other girls parted their legs too for this dumb son of a bitch, and they didn't have to marry him. Those stupid bitches! They were the ones who encouraged her in the first place to visit the swine-herd boy at the village boundary where he herds his filthy pigs. They said he was not very smart, not very handsome, but his tool is rock hard, and he always carries some wine in his shoulder bag. He's not good for anything else, but he's a proper candidate to lose her virginity to. But she would never have imagined that, along with her virginity, she could lose herself, too. She did it out of curiosity; she was planning to send the boy to Hell at the very last minute, then she would just laugh into his face when the time came. But the alcohol got into her head quickly, and the next thing she remembered was that they were rolling in the mud together, in the dirty cloud of the pig smell, and the guy's pale ass was jumping up and down as he was banging her deeper and deeper into the slob, down, down, maybe straight to Hell, from where she hasn't returned since. Already that night, the swine-herd boy grumbled proudly in the pub that he had fucked the old tailor's girl, which of course eventually reached her father's ears. *If you have fucked with the boy, you must marry him.* Although it cost all his savings, her father paid for the wedding, for the house, and for everything—the marriage had to be concluded. She knew her father wanted to punish her, as if he was saying: if you weren't disgusted to let this boy inside you, then never let him out of you.

The swelling coral reef of the night—in this place all happiness grows only one millimeter a year. The light tentacles of the streetlamp infiltrating between the gaps of the venetian blinds are scanning the thoughts of the girl lying in the bed. The swine-herd boy next to her snores so loudly it suppresses the yowlings of the dogs in the yard. I hate him, but still I want his baby, she thinks. She needs someone around who she can love, or at least suffer with. Then they can share this torment like a tub of cold water that can never be drained. Since the first week of their marriage, she decided she wanted a child from her new husband, and they have been trying ever since, without any success. But last week, the Nest-Headed Midwife arrived, and she promised the Human Stork would come to them.

"But whatever he brings," she said, pointing a gnarled tree-like finger at the sky, "You have to breathe for the child!"

The minutes wander slowly. The dream is a distant, rocking buoy to which she could by no means swim close. The Human Stork is in her mind, maybe he will arrive tonight and bring a gift in his beak.

"What the fuck are you doing here?" she yelled at the old woman who showed up in their yard more than a week ago. The witch, dressed in dirty, torn rags was standing slantwise on the ground like a half-pulled, rotting tooth. How can anyone stand like that without tumbling face forward into the dirt? This question raced through her mind when she first saw her. The old woman leaned too far forward, her body slanting at an angle of fifty degrees to the ground. Normal people do not stand that way, they would be pulled into the dust by gravity. The old hag just stood there like she was about to kiss the ground. Next, she threw her head, adorned with tree branches, against the sky and looked; she stared increasingly at the roof, but there was no appearance of a dead stork, yet. Then in a hoarse voice she said, "I have been called, so I came. Although we haven't met yet, I have to say, those who never saw me before know me the best. I'm the Nest-Headed Midwife. I know you've heard of me, everyone in the area has."

At first, nothing came to the girl's mind, but then it flashed, like when someone finds an old black and white photo at the bottom of the drawer. Yes, yes, she had heard that name as a child. The old women in the village mentioned her a few times, just the good old tall tales and legends, which should not be taken too seriously. They were also the ones who constantly mumbled about the evil spirits, such as the one called Garabonciás, the fearsome ghost that knocks on the doors of houses asking for milk, and if he doesn't get it, he brings freezing rain or summons dragons. Silly children's tales, the attic is full of them in this countryside.

These superstitious old women said that the Nest-Headed Midwife brings child blessing to the house. She wanders across the village border, feeding on the meat of dead stray dogs. Her cataract eyes are like balls made of mercury. While she scrolls dark spells in her head, the torn wings of dragonflies rustle behind her wrinkled forehead. Her hair has twigs in it that she stole from stork nests. She searches and seeks couples who desperately want a child but don't succeed.

No, this old woman is not the legendary Nest-Headed Midwife, just some fool, was the girl's very first thought. *I'll send her the fuck away,* was her second. But then the witch stepped in front of her and she was instantly struck by the cold that leaked out from the woman's pores, and the scent of rotten liver dumpling soup that flowed from her like an evil genie.

"Of course, just send me away, you stupid bitch!" She grinned, showing her gray, gravel-like teeth. "But you should know, I never show up around the same place twice. If they send me away from somewhere, I won't return. I walk the world and bring child blessings to houses. This has been the case since the world has begun, and I will do so even when you will be lying in your coffin with the worms chewing up the remnants of your body while there will be no one left to bring flowers to your grave. You're stupid because you think a baby will lift you up and save you, but newborn bones are too fragile to hold you as you try to climb out of a pit. But I didn't come to talk you out of it... I have an offer. If you nod, a child will arrive to this house. It is not me who will bring the baby, that's the job of the Human Stork, but I'm the one who can summon him. But remember, whatever he brings, you have to breathe for the child! So, I'm asking you, girl, because the swine-herd boy doesn't care about anything, and to be honest, he doesn't even actually breathe for himself: do you want the child?"

She wanted it. More than anything. So she nodded.

The old woman replied, "All right. Then, let's get to work, we have to murder a stork!"

At noon, the swine-herd boy returned home from driving his pigs and finds a nest-headed witch sitting at the kitchen table. She ordered him to kill a stork, saw off its wings, and lay it on the roof. Then she placed a liqueur glass in front of the boy.

"What are we drinking to, grandma?" the swine-herd boy asked.

"Oh, you can drink to whatever you want!" The witch grinned. "But I suggest you do it from another glass because you have to milk your spunk into this one."

"Why did you let this old bitch in?" the lad asked his wife.

With downcast eyes she replied, "I want a child. Do you?"

The boy shrugged. Then he picked up the tiny glass and went out to the pigsty to squeeze his cock out, because he realized he doesn't really care. If he has to kill a bird, he'll do it. If he has to jerk his dick, he'll do that too. And hopefully they will just leave him be after that, he thought as his mind exploded into tiny pieces by the blinding flash of a pig-scream orgasm right there in that pigsty.

The popping blood blisters of magic. The company marched out into the yard, where the swine-herd boy aimed his gun and shot down a nesting stork from a pillar. The wounded wader bird squirmed in pain for a while, clapping its beak, splashing the arriving boy with drops of blood. It still held a few branches between its claws, which it pulled out of its nest as it fell. The witch pulled out one and inserted it into her own hair, enriching her nest wig. The swine-herd boy, following the instructions of the old hag lurking beside him, then sawed off both of the dead bird's wings, smeared its beak with his own semen and tossed up the bird onto the roof with a shovel.

"You know this is not how kids are made?" he growled at his wife.

But the girl just looked at him sharply and replied, "Oh really? Well, fucking doesn't seem to work…"

"It's the bait that will lure the Human Stork here," the old witch explained before leaving. "And when he comes, he will bring a baby with him. But the child will not be able to breathe alone." The blood-colored sunset sucked up the old woman's outlines as she left, like how a thirsty carpet slurps up the spilled-out tea, leaving only a dry stain on the girl's memory.

They haven't seen the old woman since then. The dead bird has been lying on the roof ever since, and the Human Stork hasn't arrived, yet.

"Where do babies come from?" the girl had asked her mother when she was a child, to which she replied, "Some from here, some from there... You'll find out when you grow up."

"All children don't come from the same place?"

"Some come from a better, some from a worse place," her mother explained, and she left it at that.

If the Human Stork brings my child, where will he or she come from? she wondered, but quickly realized it was foolish to think about such things. Meanwhile, more than a week had passed and nothing had changed. *It was all humbug, the old woman was exactly what she looked like, a lunatic,* she thought to herself. She would allow the boy take the corpse off the roof with his rake in the morning.

When she finally falls asleep, she dreams of this scene. The rungs of the ladder crackle painfully as the swine-herd boy climbs over them, with the rake in his hand. Loud knocks come from the roof as the tool rattles on the tiles.

"Got it!" her husband shouts in this dream, but what he pulls off from the roof is not a dead bird at all, but the tiny body of a withered, mummified baby. The lifeless child slams into the yard with a soft thud, like a tiny meteorite, raising a little dust cloud.

"Poor thing can weigh only as much as a bread," the girl thinks. She's just staring at the event in silent shock, then begins to scream as the waiting stray dogs throw themselves at the child, sinking their teeth into the helpless small dead body. In a few moments, the growling beasts are fighting over the intestines.

"My baby!" she roars, and the frescoes of hope crack and fall to the ground in pieces. At the top of the ladder, the swine-herd boy just laughs.

"Let the hounds have it!" His laughter is like a kick up a beehive, as angry stingrays begin to poke the clouds.

"My baby..."

And then, from who knows where, the stern voice of the witch creeps in like a winding insect, crawling right into her ear canal.

"It's your fault, you little bitch! You didn't breathe for the child!"

~

THE NOISE of clapping beaks pulls her out of this terrible dream. As her eyes pop open her forehead collides with the black block wall of the night. It's still a long way 'til morning. Some stray dogs are barking in the yard, while her husband snores next to her as if a pig is grunting, but she heard, she really heard that clapping sound beyond this awful snarl.

The girl's first thought is that the dead stork thrown on the roof had somehow come back to life. She imagines the torn-winged bastard writhing over their heads like an angry worm. You killed me, but I came back from the dead and I will pierce your heart with my sharp beak—maybe that's what it's trying to say. She puts her hand over her mouth, but the scream is unstoppable, it struggles upward through her throat, and she imagines if she doesn't give it a free way, a tiny gap will appear on her forehead, from where it can flow out into the world. Suddenly she hears that noise again. Yes, clapping, but it doesn't come from the roof, but from the yard, from the hungry throat of the night.

"Wake up!" she squeaks, but realizes she's still squeezing his mouth with her palm. She takes her hand away and repeats the sentence. The sleeping swine-herd boy doesn't even hear her words. The girl gives him a good hard kick in the thigh as he attempts to snore again. She gives his thigh a hard kick once again and her husband stops snoring.

"Wake up!" the girl cries.

"What the fuck?" her husband mutters, but then he hears the noise too, as if bones clink together rhythmically over and over again, as if the teeth of every damned soul were chattering at once down there in Hell, which is perhaps not full of flames but filled with the indelible cold of fear. The girl digs her teeth into her own wrist when she realizes the frightening beak-clapping noise is coming from a closer place, not from the yard, but directly from the front door.

"He has arrived," she mutters.

"That's impossible," the boy replies.

"The Human Stork has arrived, and..." But she can only finish the sentence in her thoughts.

"May-maybe he'll ju-just go away if we don't op-open the door!" her husband stutters, and the girl immediately forgets all of her fears and only anger remains in her soul. This feeling of irritation and hatred swoops her with such a force that she becomes dizzy. Her stomach twitches and nausea begins to strangle her throat.

"You fucking bastard!" That's all she can squeeze out between her trembling lips. "This is what we were waiting for!"

"What you were waiting for?" the boy asks, burying his face in his hands. "I wasn't waiting for anything."

"Because you never want anything." The springs in the mattress squeak as she jumps out of bed. "I just wanted a baby, but you are so worthless, you're not even able to give me one. I bet secretly you are fucking your dirty pigs, wasting your semen on them! But you know what? I couldn't care less. The Human Stork is here and he brought me my baby!"

The voice in front of the door sounds like that of a kitten. "Please don't open the door," he begs, but she knows that's exactly what she's going to do. She will let the Human Stork right into this house, because she hates this poor excuse of a man from the bottom of her heart, this cowardly bug that moved into her bed and crawled into her warm little life, and since then it has only been writhing on its back, scratching the air helplessly with its jointed legs.

Again, the sound of clapping. She takes careful steps in the dark house, hugging herself with her cold arms, thinking, *He brought my baby, the old woman didn't lie.*

"I'll make you a baby, a real one, just don't let that thing in!" the swine-herd boy moans somewhere from the bedroom, but she doesn't let herself get distracted. There's no knocking, just clapping, but she knows the Human Stork is standing right in front of the damned front door that has slammed on her life for a year and a half, and he indeed wants to get in. Where do babies come from? Well, of course, the Human Stork brings them, so it's time to open that frigging door. He arrived with a happy little package.

I have to turn on the light, I just can't do this in the dark, she decides. Her fingers are already searching for the switch. After a few moments, a strong light fills the kitchen, and the very sight of the furniture, which usually made her sad and disgusted, feels quite pleasant and reassuring now: everything's all right, these usual contours say.

But wait, maybe the light will scare away the Human Stork, she realizes. Yes, yes, it's more than possible, because this whole thing is a dream, and such things vanish instantly into nothingness in a well-lighted, casual kitchen where there's only room for sad sighs and real worries.

This thought fills her with fear rather than relief. It's a sure sign that she needs to open that door. But the guest is apparently not disturbed by the light coming from the kitchen. The excited clapping rises again, she feels as if her bones are toasting with each other deep in her flesh to the newcomer.

Enough, she decides and jumps to the door. She knows she can't wait any longer, that she has to open it fast because if she does it slowly, by the end of the move she'll lose the power of will, and she will regret for the rest of her life that she hadn't invited in the guest. She turns the key in the lock and then steps back, pressing her hand to her chest as if she has touched something hot. Silence ensues, and only the pounding sounds of her heart beating in her throat, the words of entreaty coming out from the bedroom, and the distant dog howls and pig snorts can be heard.

"You can come in, it's open," she mutters uncertainly to the door. There's no response.

I'm such a fool, she thinks. *There's nobody out there.* But deep down, she knows this is not true. He's out there, but she has to let him in, she has to open the door for him, there's no other solution.

So she steps forward and spins her fingers on the door-knob, then opens the door.

Where do babies come from?

She swallows back the nascent scream that is forming in her throat and begins to back away by the time the Human Stork, as if just following the choreography of some silly ballroom dance, enters the kitchen with the package in his hand. The stench of this strange old man immediately takes possession of the space, like fermented corn, and suddenly it's everywhere, all over, pushing out the air in the room. The body of the naked figure is all covered with light gray, dry mud, with only his arms being black. He looks even older than the witch herself. His skin hangs like dough under the peel of the mud layer. He holds dark river shells in his toothless mouth, clicking them together between his gums to mimic the clapping sounds of a stork. Every time the shells in his withered mouth knock, the girl's heart misses a beat. The man wanders slowly in, his tiny penis striking against his limp thighs with every step taken. His eyes are black holes, just burn marks in his face. The girl suddenly realizes that his two arms look so dark because the mud on them is still wet, but on the rest of his body the dirt is all dried and more pale. He looks like he's been digging the ground with his bare hands all night. But she tries not to focus on those hands, not on those chitin-like ugly nails, and not on those pitch-black eye sockets, but on the package that he holds between his fingers: the dirty bundle of rags, the gift.

She trembles all over her body, her fingers carving in her own palm, the kaleidoscope of terror tearing her thoughts to swirling shreds. She tries to greet her scary guest, but the old man starts clicking the shells in his mouth and then places the package on the floor with slow movements. The girl wants to rush to the rag bundle, but her mind protests against getting too close to the Human Stork. Fortunately, the old man apparently does not want to enjoy her hospitality for long. As soon as he places the package on the floor, he turns around and starts out the door, clapping farewells while chewing on the shells.

"Thank you!" the girl shouts after him, but the Human Stork either does not hear or he doesn't care. After squatting out of the house, he disappears behind the dark curtain of the night.

The girl looks at the gift left on the kitchen floor for long seconds. She takes a deep breath and descends on all fours.

"Baby. My dear baby," she mutters.

"What the hell is that?" The question comes from behind her. The swine-herd boy is standing there in his junky pajamas, with a snow-white face, watching the bundle in shock.

"The Human Stork brought me my baby!" she grins, her fingers already untying the rag. But when she unfolds it, she begins to scream. The blood rushes out from her face and she throws herself back, even beating her head at the foot of the dining table. A new kind of stench rises up in the air, and it's more stomach-turning than the smell of the Human Stork. In the middle of the rag lies the rotting baby, its skin almost black, strange mucus dripping from its cavities. His tiny eyelids are moving like those of the dreaming people, but behind them slimy worms are clinging to each other.

"It's dead!" The swine-herd boy whines and vomits immediately. The swelling sail of horror. The folded meat of nightmares. Where do babies come from? Some from a better, some from a worse place. The girl suddenly remembers the filthy hands of the Human Stork. It was like he'd been digging the ground with his bare hands all night.

No, this is a mistake, it must be!

She wants to scream, but when she opens her mouth wide, she feels her throat tighten as her most painful shout tries to struggle to the surface. All of a sudden she runs out of air. Her lungs begin to constrict and are unable to squeeze out any sound beyond pathetic whimpering. She's starting to choke. At first she thinks the stench of decay is suffocating her, that the ugly smell is squeezing the air out of her. But then she remembers the old woman's words. Whatever the Human Stork brings, you have to breathe for the child!

Air! she screams inside her skull and tries to breathe through her mouth and nose at the same time. And suddenly, the dead baby's tiny chest rises. Just a little bit. Then again and again. The girl presses her hand to her own chest and feels she is breathing with the baby. As she tries to take deeper breaths, only a few get into her own lungs. It feels like she is halving every breath she takes with the child.

"No..." she groans, but she's unable to form the word normally from this thirst for air.

No, no, no, she thinks. *I'm not ready to be a mother, I don't have enough air to share with the baby. I didn't know that becoming a parent was like this!*

The baby slowly opens its eyes and white cataract beads sparkle in the brightness radiating from the kitchen lamp. From behind the baby's eyelids some white worms drop to the floor like tears. Then the newborn begins to cry, filling the kitchen with its grave-smelling breath. As its voice grows stronger and stronger, it uses all of her mother's breath for this afterlife wail and the girl begins to grab her own throat. Meanwhile something heavy falls on her chest like cement. She realizes she'll never breathe properly again.

MORTON COTTAGE

BY LEEROY CROSS JAMES

I t was the dream home—the perfect location—for John Hastings. He'd been wanting to escape back to the country for some time. The listing seemed persuasive enough: *one-bedroomed cottage in a rural area, close to town with a stunning view of the local church.* The words John used when he and Derek finally viewed the cottage in person were "charming" and "secluded." Derek kept quiet. He thought those two words couldn't be any further apart from the context John attempted to use them in. Even the narrow, gritted lane they drove up made Derek feel claustrophobic, and this was before they'd even entered the property.

The estate agent, Rebecca, really played up to John's childlike fascination with just about everything inside. Wide eyes, extensive grins, and lengthy nods took over as Rebecca showed one bare room after another. Derek didn't get the appeal of exposed brickwork, peeling matt emulsion and outdated kitchen fittings, but the worn-out look seemed to seduce John.

"It'll be nice and quiet for you both," Rebecca said, shifting her eyes from John to Derek, as if she was checking he was paying attention. Derek offered a weak smile, feeling like he was back in the classroom. "I'm sure from what you've told me, it's exactly what you've been looking for. Plus, your neighbors are a bit further out, so you'd more or less have the area to yourselves."

In actual fact, Morton Cottage was the only property on Morton Lane, there weren't any other properties nearby at all. That was the first thing Derek noticed when they drove up the pathway. Overgrown greenery, weeds and an abundance of dandelion clocks invaded either side of the cottage.

"It hasn't exactly been well kept, has it?" Derek asked, which provoked a small nudge in the ribs from John. But that didn't stop him from continuing. "It's been on the market a while, so what's the catch?"

Before Rebecca could answer, John steered the conversation in a different direction. "Could you show us the back garden?"

While John followed Rebecca out the backdoor, Derek waited in the living room. Nothing more to see—nothing worth raving about at least. The front of the cottage intrigued him more than anything else. He stared out the front window and there it was—as promised in the listing: the church. If they put an offer in to buy the place, they'd have a full view of the building, especially the steeple. What the listing failed to mention was that the cottage faced a cemetery that tacked onto the back of the Methodist Church. With only the narrow path between the cottage driveway and the iron gate, it was practically on the cottage doorstep. *Charming? Bloody morbid more like.*

"Think of it as inspiration," John said from behind, breaking Derek out of his trance. He joined him to look at the view. "This will be the perfect place to come out of hiatus, don't you think?"

Although he didn't need reminding by his own husband—because the weekly emails from his agent were enough—Derek hadn't written a word in two years. He was aware he needed to get back in the game, the mortgage more or less would rely on it. He nodded in agreement, not entirely convinced or fussed on the cottage, but John made it clear he really wanted it.

Derek sighed. "Well, it's quiet enough," he said, resting his arm around John's waist. "Perhaps it will bring some inspiration."

It was the closest thing to "yes" that John was going to get. He wandered off to let Rebecca know they were putting in an offer. Alone again, Derek felt a draft on his neck that made him shrug his shoulders up as far as they would go to cover his bare, freezing skin.

When they finished the viewing, Rebecca waved them off as they walked to the car. As soon as Derek opened the door, a lightning-fast shape of black fur darted from underneath the car. He stumbled backward into a puddled pothole.

"Jesus!" Derek yelled, watching it sprint off.

John raced around from the passenger's side to help him up. "What? What was it?"

"A bloody cat!"

A MONTH in Morton Cottage and Derek already missed the apartment—and the city. Not just because he was constantly freezing, but the hot water only lasted a minute in the ancient shower. Then there was the garden. No matter what he used to prevent it, or how often he painstakingly cleared up the overgrown weeds around the sides of the cottage, they continued to grow back in no time. The writing didn't come easily after all, and out of boredom, Derek found a pastime—spying outside. No one ever came down Morton Lane, despite it being a shortcut into town. Most days he observed the sandstone wall around the perimeter of the cemetery. There was a tabby cat who had spent the past two weeks lazing on the wall, bathing himself to his heart's content. One rainy afternoon, he continued to rest there, despite the spitting rainfall. The tabby-tom had company.

"There's two of them now," Derek said, holding back the net curtain.

John emerged from the kitchen. "Let's have a look, then," he said, resting his chin on Derek's shoulder. "Fascinating. Why don't you sign up for neighbourhood watch? Your first suggestion can be that all our neighbours should keep their cats indoors."

Derek completely missed the joke. "They're strays. Look, no collars."

"Not necessarily," John said. "It is strange though; you hardly ever see cats out and about like you used to."

"I bet they're vicious little bastards, too."

"Not all cats are like that, Derek."

Derek pointed to the clear, thin scar on the back of his neck. "That tabby, he looks just like the one who did that."

"You were ten, mate." John couldn't help it. He giggled at how serious Derek looked. "Get over it."

"Even his markings are the same..."

Bored of the conversation, John walked back toward the kitchen. As he passed Derek's laptop, he read the single word on the screen: *BOOK*. "Are you actually going to do some work today or are you just going to continue curtain-twitching?"

Not listening to the question, Derek nodded, still fixated

on the wall outside.

The cats stopped bathing and stood like guarding statues on either side of the iron gate. *How very Poe.* They'd clocked Derek staring at them and returned his curiosity.

The feline hissed, while the tabby-tom's stare became a frown.

THAT NIGHT, huffing and puffing since his head hit the pillow, Derek jumped out of bed to do some work. Insomnia was like an old friend that came to visit a little more often than Derek liked—especially since they'd moved into the cottage. The last good night's sleep he'd had was at the apartment, but he just put that down to being in new surroundings. Caffeine probably wasn't the best choice, seeing as it was nearly 3 a.m., but Derek used to get his best writing done late at night, and sleep probably wouldn't come to him if he continued lying in bed. Before he could even type the first word, he heard a prolonged wailing from outside.

That bloody cat.

Derek peeked through the nets. It was pitch black. There were no streetlamps on Morton Lane, and they were yet to purchase a sensor light for the front door. It was on the to-do list—along with a million other things the cottage needed. The fantasy of living in an ancient cottage was more appealing than the reality. It was John's project though, he was the fixer-upper, more artsy one in the relationship, and he had grand ideas to make Morton Cottage more homey for both of them.

As much as Derek tried to ignore it, the cat—wherever it was—continued crying. It was so agonizing to listen to.

Derek guessed it was probably mate-calling from how heightened the moaning was. The cries were that loud that they lingered in Derek's ears like a case of tinnitus. He was surprised the racket hadn't woken John up. The more it annoyed him, the more high-pitched the cries became. After several minutes, he'd had enough. Derek slid on his boots, grabbed the torch from the kitchen and rushed out the front door. He had no idea what he was going to do once he saw it. *Try to scare it away?* If it didn't scare him first, that is.

The wall was vacant and the lane was empty. Derek even checked under the car after the incident on viewing day, and it sounded close enough. *Maybe the little shit heard the front door open and bolted?* Before giving up and returning indoors, the cat's next call confirmed its location. Derek sighed. *Of course.* Thank God he had a torch, because he wouldn't have braved passing the flimsy iron gate to the cemetery in the middle of the night otherwise.

Derek cringed as the wet sludgy mud seeped through the lining of his boots. The ground was moist, and he could smell the earth with each step he took. Despite the squelching sensation inside his shoes, he continued to walk the path, guided by the yellow glow of his torch. The calling became louder; the cat was nearby. He flashed his torch along the moss-covered tombstones that towered to about half his height. More green than gray, and barely readable from the rain damage over the years—well, century—they appeared more like props in a gothic creature feature. The spurts of dandelion clocks instead of flowers only added to the macabre effect. He spun round, flashing his light in the opposite direction. He heard leaves crunching, but there was nothing but more tombstones.

"*Ch-ch-ch,*" he chanted in the empty pathway, looking and feeling a little bit ridiculous. *Do cats even respond to such sounds?* No movement or trotting could be seen or heard as he carried on. *Evidentially not.* The cat's crying had stopped altogether.

"Where are you, you little bastard?"

Nothing but the occasional car driving along the road on the other side of the church provided the soundtrack to the night. *Probably scared the little bugger away.* Derek made tracks back to the cottage, his feet now soggy and sopping from the damp. Aided by the torch, he saw the iron gate up ahead, but pulled to a halt when the light revealed a row of holographic dots sprinkled against the night's dark canvas. He dared himself to lift the light just a tad higher. There must have been seven... eight—no—there were *ten* cats resting on the sandstone wall. Different breeds and colours of cat all stared at him, patiently shifting their tails. *Where did they all come from?* Their calm stance confused him. It seemed absurd. They all seemed... organised. Like they had been awaiting his arrival.

It was silly, but he was scared to walk past them. Scared to move at all. There appeared to be no pleasantries with these cats. In fact, the cross frowns on their furry faces indicated that they were anything but pleasant. The chilling thing was, other than their tails, they didn't move or flinch. Not a cock of the head, a lick of the paw—nothing. He wasn't prepared to camp out in the cold, damp cemetery for the night.

"Fun's fun, but to *hell* with bloody nonsense!" he said, giving himself some courage. He walked only a few steps, then a chorus of angry growls began.

The cats started to jump down onto the cemetery ground, descending like soldiers ready to seize and attack. It made Derek pick up the pace, but they all trotted toward him, hissing and growling. One swiped at his legs, deep into his skin. Thanks to the cold air, the wound stung instantly. His own retaliation was to kick his leg out between short sprints, which made some scatter away.

"Go on, piss off!" he yelled.

Behind him, he could still hear the growls, the hisses and their tiny footsteps sloosh into the mud. Ahead, the living room light came on in the cottage. Derek ran through the door, breathless. Even after being smoke-free for nearly three years, he still couldn't run for long without coughing.

John stormed into the hall, his hair in tufts, naked from the waist up. "Derek, it's past three in the morning," he said with squinted eyes. "Where the bloody hell have you been?"

Should he lie? Tell the truth? Either way, Derek couldn't deny that it was unusual behaviour to leave the house in the middle of the night without saying so. Once he got his breath back, he leaned against the wall.

"I was just attacked by a pack of cats." The moment the words came out of his mouth, he winced. He knew how ludicrous it sounded—and was.

First it was confusion on his sleepy face, then John crossed his arms. Derek didn't even need him to say anything, he could read him like a book. "What are you on about?"

"I heard that tabby crying outside—or, at least, I thought it was the tabby," Derek began. "I went to chase it off, because it was driving me nuts, crying. Then I saw a pack of them, just sitting on the wall. And they attacked me." He pulled up his trouser leg and revealed a pathetic scratch. "Look."

John stared at his leg for a moment. Eventually, he nodded. "I'm going back to bed," he whispered and turned back toward the bedroom, shaking his head.

"John?" Derek called out. John poked his head back out

the door frame. "I swear to you, that's what happened."

John nodded again. "Get some sleep," he mumbled, and disappeared back into the bedroom, slamming the door behind him.

Derek pressed his ear against the front door.

Outside, it was silent for the rest of the night.

A RAINY DAY. The *tic-tac* of raindrops hitting the roof. Derek was grateful, otherwise the silence between himself and John would have been unbearable. He should have been thinking about his next novel—he should have written at least a chapter by that afternoon—but the events of the night before were still on his mind. John put it down to simple paranoia, and even suggested that he move his office desk into the bedroom. That way he wouldn't be tempted to look out the window every couple of minutes to see if any cats were there. It wasn't paranoia that was plaguing Derek's thoughts—he was spooked by what he saw.

"I'm going to make a sandwich," John said, abruptly. Derek even jumped a little bit. It wasn't often John was short with him. However, they had been more disconnected than they ever had been before since moving to Morton Cottage. There wasn't much laughter between them anymore.

Derek didn't reply, just nodded.

"Do you want one or not?" John asked.

"No, thank you."

Instead of storming off, like he'd done for most of that day, John plonked himself onto the comfort chair, grabbing his face with both hands. "I'm exhausted," he mumbled through his fingers. Derek knew that he didn't mean from lack of sleep.

"I think it was a mistake moving here," Derek managed, swallowing the lump in his throat. "Do you not feel it?'"

John crossed his brows. "Feel what, exactly? This is the problem, Derek, you don't tell me what you feel. *Ever.*"

Derek considered the comment for a moment, and even hesitated in giving the truthful answer—the right answer. He was very aware of how difficult he was, especially when it came to the move in general, but he didn't want to make John's life difficult. "This place has a bad energy; it doesn't feel right to be here."

"You're just tired," John whispered, rolling his eyes. "When was the last time you actually had a good night's sleep?" He looked over at the screen on Derek's laptop. "That's why you can't write anything."

Of course, he would bring up Derek's insomnia. Next it would be accusations of erratic behaviour, then anger, and finally depression. John had a habit of diagnosing Derek's "spells," but this time that wasn't the case.

"We need to leave."

"Don't be ridiculous, Derek!" John had heard enough, he jumped up from the chair and started to walk away but stopped. "Perhaps it's not the cottage that's the problem, perhaps it's just you. They're cats, not fucking monsters. Grow up!"

When John left the room, Derek huffed and turned to the laptop. Banging at the keys furiously, he wrote:

I hate this fucking house. I hate this fucking house. I fucking hate this house.

I fucking hate cats.

FOR THE FIRST night in a long time, Derek was confined to the couch. The argument hadn't been resolved at all, and John even ate dinner in the bedroom instead of at the kitchen table. Derek hadn't eaten a thing all day, but he wasn't hungry. He looked out the window throughout the day, but neither the tabby-tom or his friends from the night before had been there all day. He hoped that was the last he would see—or hear—of them.

Derek managed to sleep for an hour or so, after plenty of tossing and turning on the sinking cushions of the couch. When he looked at his phone it had just gone past 3 a.m. It wasn't spontaneous that he woke up from his short rest. It was the scratching that came from the front door.

The nearest thing he could grab was an old fire poker. He marched straight to the front door and pulled it open. It started to rain—it crashed down on him like hard tiny stones. Without a moment's hesitation, he banged the poker onto the front step, repeatedly smacking it against the concrete. Even when he was aware there was nothing there, he continued to hit the step. The hollow beating echoed throughout the lane.

"Derek?" John called behind him. "What the *fuck* are you doing?"

It was useless trying to pull Derek back into the house, he was too strong for John to handle. The sound of the iron smacking the concrete was that loud that Derek couldn't even hear John's pleas to stop. It was only when the poker made contact with something behind him that Derek did stop. He saw the silhouette of his husband, grabbing his left shoulder in the hallway. It gave him a clue where the poker landed.

Derek was frantic. "I'm sorry, I didn't mean to—"

"What the hell is wrong with you?" John winced from the pain. "You need help!"

Derek tried to make a fuss and applied his hand to John's shoulder, but John quickly pulled it away and headed to the kitchen. The light in there revealed the bloody gash just below his collarbone that leaked down his bare chest. John grabbed a kitchen towel and applied pressure to the wound.

"I'll drive you to the hospital," Derek said. "You're going to need stitches."

All John gave him was a spiteful glare. The more he pressed the towel onto his wound, the more his breathing became heavy from the pain and panic. Derek was full of guilt, that was apparent enough to John, but he couldn't cope with his behaviour any longer. "I want you to leave. Right now."

"I'm not leaving you like this!"

John barged past Derek, using his good shoulder, and grabbed his car keys from the kitchen table. "Fine," he said, "I'll leave, then."

Derek followed John. The front door was still wide open, and the rain had come down so heavy that it flooded the pathway. John's bare feet sank into the puddles on their drive, right up to his ankles. When he reached the car, he made a point of slamming the door as hard as he could when he got inside. As soon as he turned on the ignition, and the headlights came on, John froze. In a flash, they appeared like apparitions in front of the headlights and their holographic eyes glowed from the light.

They were along the wall, on the path, the drive and some even rested on top of the car. The rain didn't bother them, even though it soaked their fur. They were patiently waiting. This wasn't just a group; it was an army. Derek couldn't believe his eyes; he wasn't going insane—and now John could see them, too. One weak, small *meow* from the tabby-tom, who sat in his usual space on the sandstone, began the chorus of what seemed like a thousand cats calling out to Derek and John.

The ones resting on the car began to claw at the soft top. John revved the engine, hoping it would scare them off, but it only made them more feral. The moment Derek took a step toward the car, the cats turned their attention to him. Like little beasts, they hissed and snarled at him, boxing their paws into the air.

John got out of the car.

Derek's eyes widened. "John, get back inside. *Now!*"

"I'm not afraid of a bunch of fucking cats!"

The tabby-tom jumped onto John's back and clawed at his neck—an invitation for the others to join in. Their open claws hit him from all directions. John screamed out in pain and fell to the ground as they weighed him down. More leapt onto him, and eventually Derek could no longer see John at all, only a nest of wet fur.

Muffled screams and cries for help came from under the fur.

Derek couldn't. He just couldn't do it. "I'm sorry..."

The tabby-tom emerged from the nest. The headlights on the car showed the sleek red that covered its face like warpaint, which the rain quickly washed away. *Blood. John's blood.* It walked gracefully toward the cottage.

Derek ran back inside and slammed the door behind him. He closed his eyes and pressed his palms into his ears to shield the gurgling screams of his husband.

When John's screams stopped, the cats scratched at the door.

JUNIPER'S SPRING
BY DANIEL WILLCOCKS

Juniper Fallow stalked the silent streets, large jar cupped in her delicate hands.

Her bare feet padded the stone pavement, not a decibel raised. Eyes fixed to the darkening sky as the sun set and the belly of peach fuzz turned to shades of a day-old bruise.

Not a soul was in sight. Not a shopkeeper winding down from their daily duties, not a stray wanderer racing their way home, not a modicum of smog-choked traffic on the roads.

Just a solitary little girl, straight-walking through the center of town, aiming for the high-sloping hills beyond.

She was too young to be out here alone. Eleven years old with the weight of a thousand winters behind keen hazel eyes. Her hair was cropped at her shoulders, snipped in jagged clumps of her own doing. She wore a nightgown, moth-bitten at the seams, soil-stained where the reaches of the thin cotton brushed at her knees. Her skin was pallid, and anyone who stood in their windows that day watching the girl pass by would have been forgiven for mistaking her for a long-dead ghoul.

Her arms shook beneath the strain, nothing more than thin brambles wet with tissue paper, clinging to her skeleton. Her skin sank like market stall canvas sodden with rain.

And, still, she walked.

She didn't blink. She hardly breathed. The jar in her hands was heavy, weighted by the dark substance at its bottom, but her white-knuckle grip maintained as she passed her first kilometer from her hovel of a home, then two, then three. The city center shrank away, bleeding into rows of picturesque houses better suited to a Disney film. Perfectly manicured front lawns, pristine, gleaming windows, the scent of home baking lingering in the air, ovens and dinners forgotten by their owners as the inhabitants of the city shrank away and hid themselves in their dark hollows. Families piled into closets, lovers suffocated beneath sheets. A whole world waited on the brink of a single trembling breath as the impossible worked its course past their abodes.

One impossible girl.

One impossible action.

One impossible night.

The city knew not why they hid. Mother instinct buries deep into the genealogy of creatures; the mouse has no real understanding of why it scurries ahead of the swooping owl, the daffodils have no real knowledge of why they must bloom in the spring, the cicadas know not why they crest the dirt and fornicate for the survival of their species on the anniversary of seventeen long years passed, and not a second before.

Seasons are arbitrary.

Knowledge is only a weapon in the hands of the Greats.

The lamb shivers before the slaughter, unable to voice or identify the threat until blood is spilled and life drains freely.

And there she walked, a single girl in the channels of the Greats, padding her way uphill. A lamb offering herself to the chopping block.

The land rose before her, cobble and asphalt fading to grass. Grass fading to dirt to grass to dirt. Stones bit her feet, keen leaven blades left red stripes on her ankles, and still she walked, climbing ever higher as the world shrank below and she approached the darkening sky. Magic thrummed in the sky that night, great cotton candy clouds catching the purple fuzz of dusk and turning the air sweet. Somewhere in the distant beyond something fizzed and crackled, Juniper's gossamer hairs standing to attention like obedient soldiers.

Her breath caught.

She choked.

She coughed.

Her stomach rumbled.

She climbed.

Horses gave way to her presence, shrinking away to the safe confines of the oaks, beetle-black eyes tracking her movements as they silently stood and quaked. Not a bird to be seen in the sky. Not a bat or a bug dared swoop or breathe a word.

Still, she climbed.

~

"Something's coming."

The old man's gaze tracked the young girl, her movements light, floating like a specter across the cobbles.

"Something big."

Eyes narrowed through the daisy lace curtains, the girl slipping from sight. In the distance, a great cloth of gray raced toward them, dragging the night in its wake. He glanced at his watch, noticed the hands had stopped moving. A glance at his bedside digital clock showed flashing digits displaying only zeroes. Just an arm's width away, Abigail lay silently in bed.

"Yes. Something's coming." He gave the outside world an affirmative nod before resuming his seat at his bedside. The mattress, which usually protested at his weight, had nothing to say. The springs which usually cracked and pinged were silent. Thomson lay his head back on the pillows and stared at the ceiling.

"Silent as the grave..." he muttered, noticing then how his words which usually echoed around the room, powered by his booming bass, failed to bounce back. No echo. No feedback. No vibration. No amplification.

His words were snatched.

An eyebrow rose.

"Looming like the beating of a moth's mighty wing. Mothra come at last." A chuckle.

He glanced at Abigail, her back turned to him. The hunch of her spine, developed over years of tending to her dozen or so fluffy pedigrees, rose like the mound of Jack's hill. How many times had he crested that mound to kiss those lips? How many years had he traipsed against gravity to snatch a morsel of affection? Whisker to whisker. Ashes to ashes.

Dust to dust.

Why? Why so morbid?

A tear traced his cheek. A smile whispered on his lips.

He lay there for some time, swimming in the viscous

quiet. The world felt heavy. The air was thick. Each breath brought with it a chill that hadn't been there before. He strained his ears as a sound—the only sound he'd heard since returning home early from work, unsure how, why, or when he had gotten back—gently rang through the room.

Not her dogs.

No, they had their own distinct voices. Growls and whines and barks. Each one speaking a language of companionship, affection, and want.

A knocking.

Quiet at first, but rapid. The gentle fire of a clockwork machine gun muted against a cloud of cotton. Thomson looked up at the ceiling, hunting for the origin of the sound. He rose from bed and followed, dreamlike, as the sound chipped again. A *rat-tat-tat* of fingers on wood. As he stalked toward the thick timber beams that supported the ancient Victorian house, images came unbidden to his mind. Skeletal fingers knocking from inside the crypt. Bony digits tapping and thrumming against the wooden hollows of their coffins, requesting permission to join the land of the living.

He wandered to Abigail's side of the bed, breath so thin it could slide beneath the doorframe. He pressed his ear to the timber, the stranger on the other side demanding entry, desperate for release, the sound rising to an incessant, constant drum roll...

Thomson ran a finger down the beam. Its surface was ice cold, the soft wood bowing beneath the minimal pressure he exuded. Where his finger traced, a groove followed, the wood rotting and crumbling away like sand until the hollow revealed inside.

Something flitted across the opening. Thomson swallowed dryly, his face the pallid shade of candle wax. The beetle crept to the exposed hole and sniffed the air.

"Lord..." Thomson breathed.

The Deathwatch beetle was no larger than his thumbnail. And as he stared at it, and it to him, it started to vibrate, body tensing as its head rocked back and forth. Without warning, the beetle drummed its brittle skull against the wood, the sound reminiscent of a woodpecker, only this rattle a thousand times louder in volume. Thomson clapped his hands to his ears, shrinking away from the beetle, falling as his legs hit the bed, collapsing back onto his wife's form, scoliosis spine bursting with a sudden white-hot jolt as the beetle continued its offensive concerto.

"Stop! Make it stop!"

Still that same notion that he was shouting to himself alone, and no one else in the world could hear him exclaim. Oh, to be heard. To feel the familial and to know that he wasn't alone in his anguish.

He sat up, lips peeled back, nose damp with viscous mucus. His eyes blurred with tears as he hunted for the beetle. The beetle quieted, as though somebody had twisted the volume dial all the way to mute. Its head and body thrashed on, skull incessantly smashing into the wood, but the sound was fading, fading...

Gone...

Thomson sat up, breathless and afraid. Something strange was happening that night, that much he already knew. What he didn't know was how or why.

Or why Abigail hadn't awoken to the sounds of his screams. Why Abigail hadn't so much as stirred since he had returned home from work to find the dogs sitting silent and obedient in their cages, ears folded back, and tails gone limp. Why Abigail hadn't breathed a feather's mote of air since he had entered the room.

And as he turned his attention to his wife of forty-three years, peacefully resting beneath the sheets, he suddenly understood.

Hand to cheek, he pressed his ear against his wife's lips. Lips to forehead he kissed his final goodbye. Heart to soul he lay beside her, his bent, aching frame perfectly resting against the hunch of her ancient spine.

And still the beetle continued its silent drumming.

AT THE TOP of the hill, Juniper paused.

The tightly packed ground beneath Juniper's feet trodden flat from years of foot traffic as the city's citizens made their way to "Lover's Leap" and looked out across the city. From here she could see everything. From here she could see Robinson's Bakers, could smell the scent of warm dough and freshly piped buttercream. From here she could see the Astrid football stadium, could hear the roaring cheers of the home crowd, rising in one colossal chorus as the ball struck the back of the away team's net. From here the cathedral spiked the sky like a monster's fang, daring the sky to come closer so that it could puncture its flesh and drain its contents upon the city, its bell vibrationless and abandoned. From here the roads twisted like ink-filled arteries, blood cell traffic frozen in time and space. From here she could see her home, a small thatch cottage on the far city limits, a shack, a joke, a lollypop cottage with holes that whistled as the wind crawled inside and sought succor—all that was left to her when it happened.

The wind licked her face, then fell still. A single tear

rolled down her cheek. Her palms sweaty, the jar slipping slowly from her grasp. Her eyes tracked the cemetery. Half a kilometer away. Bordered by a copse of guardian oaks, the desolate Baptist church dilapidated and broken.

A broken world for a broken girl.

There was something poetic to that.

Juniper sat, her legs folding into a basket as she levered herself into position. The glass jar rested in the bowl of her legs, the candy-striped lid rusted in a couple of spots around the edge. Once it had contained boiled candies, and still the scent lingered on the inner surface of the glass. She gripped the lid and unscrewed, the only sound to fill the deafening worldly silence. The scent of earth and time filled her nostrils as she stared down into the fine powdered ashes which filled the bottom third of the glass.

Her eyes stung. Tears welled. Her lip quivered. Somewhere, far off in the distance, thunder rumbled.

"Time..." she breathed. A single, hollow word that caught in her throat. The one thing she never had with her. The one thing that was stolen from the sobbing infant.

In the center of the powdered ashes, a single gem of green. A lone leaf, growing in tandem with a single yellow bud. Half an inch tall, standing in stark contrast to the blackened desert of its surroundings. It shouldn't have been there. Juniper's mother had been dead for six years. Taken in her prime, no explanation cast. A shockwave which dented and stained the chronology of her family's timeline, leaving behind Juniper and a brother who had forgotten she existed. Juniper, a ghost in her own home, a forgotten footnote in her brother's life as he lost himself to internet addiction, a room dense with body odor, molding with potato chips, hormones, a wastepaper basket filled with Kleenex and a credit card which shouted at him down the phone lines twice weekly.

Juniper needed to escape.

Juniper whispered to her mother.

Juniper saw the bud spring, twitch. A beacon of the changing seasons, if only Juniper would grasp her chance. A sign of greater things to come, that goodness can spring from devastation. That hope will supersede harrowing loss. That the dusk will always lead to the dawn.

Rainfall, now. Tiny droplets swelling into a monstrous monsoon. The ground softened, darkening in its moisture. Cotton candy clouds burned to cinders, leaving behind roiling sheets of black rolling and rumbling in the sky.

The storm had come.

No lights illuminated the city.

Only one light source remained, and it spiked down upon the town, cracking with the force of a thousand gladiator whips. Jagged lightning, splitting the sky, shattering roof tiles and seeking its bed in the earth. Juniper's hairs were painfully brittle, her skin goosefleshed as she rose to her feet, eyes fixed to the sky. Her dress clung to her malnourished skin. The rain beat the dirt off her flesh, caressing her with chilled fingers of a force unseen. She cried, sobbed, spent her tears as currency presented to the elements, eyes red and stinging with each rain drop. She offered the jar, holding it up before her on arms that shouldn't have been strong enough, but which willpower, adrenaline, and the destiny written in her blood granted her.

Lightning teased the girl. It danced around her in great, joyous crackles. Thunder beat the drums as the lightning danced, a giant's laugh amplified through the heavens, a tree splitting nearby, its trunk cracked in two, felled with titanic creaks as it parted. Another crack and the puddles spat back against the rain, fighting a losing battle. A third, and Juniper gasped, the whip of lightning so rapid and close that, for a moment, the heat scorched her. Not five feet in front of her, a crater stood, a great divot of dirt as though a monolithic mole had surfaced and tucked itself away in the blink of an eye, unsatisfied at the world it had glimpsed.

Juniper screamed at the sky.

The sky roared back.

Juniper's mouth fixed open, every last ounce of breath existing within her fragile lungs battling the thunderous din. The sky flashed a smile, its final bolt of electricity warming up before unleashing its wrath upon her.

The sky fell silent. Rain pounded the ground.

It came.

Juniper's world became white. Her hands trembled as the bolt erupted from the sky. A single, final thunder strike.

Great hands threw Juniper backward. Great fingers snatched her gravity.

She flew through the air, tumbled across the grass, dirt gathering where the rain had just washed. The jar was wrested from her thin fingers, spinning wildly out of arm's reach.

Juniper whirled, scanning in all directions. Already the rain had stopped. The thunder had hushed and the world fell silent again, thick with anticipation as she made a dash for the jar that jerked and danced at the base of a towering elm.

She snatched the lid from the ground.

She dived for the jar.

She scooped the glass and hugged it close to her body, the jar attacking her, smashing into her hollow bird ribs. Bruises would paint her body tomorrow, but for now she fought to enclose the jar, to screw the lid with hands slimed with mud and rain. Her tongue stuck out from her lips. Her teeth champed the flesh. Iron gushed her throat, and still she wrestled, still she gripped and tensed and grunted and frolicked, a dance of one girl and one impossible creation.

The lid clamped shut.

She screwed.

The jar stilled.

Juniper lay upon the grass, a ghostly corpse hugging her mother's ashes. She huffed and wheezed, struggling to find the energy to rise. She brought the glass closer, the inside now holy with etheric light as electricity danced and played and trembled. Mesmerizing. Enchanting. Her eyes tracked the shrunken bolts, a coy grin playing on her bloody lips. Faintly, as if from a thousand miles away, a storm viewed across the Atlantic, she could hear the crackle of static. And was there something in the center of her bolt? Something with eyes and a nose and lips that smiled and plumped and called her home? A gaze so deep and primal and written in her DNA that it caused her stomach to knot and flutter?

The clouds receded, the world above revealing a sparkling soup of galaxies and constellations millions of miles away. Juniper ripped her eyes from the dizzying sparks and studied the sickle moon, its edges honed and keen, dagger sharp. Its typical white hue blooded to the same pink-red that imbued her saliva and bibbed her dress.

Juniper rose to her feet, jar clutched tightly to her stomach. She glanced inside, noting the absence of the bud. The seedling receding into the dirt, damaged and destroyed by the etheric charge she held captive.

She made her way to the lip of the world, the rim of "Lover's Leap," and glanced down at the dilapidated church. Hidden somewhere in the hallowed grounds of those broken beams and timbers was her answer. Hidden somewhere amongst the broken gravestone teeth she would find her solace.

As if in unwavering agreement, the lightning bolt smashed against the side of the glass, nudging her on, pushing her in the direction in which they both knew they had to tread.

What other choice did she have?

THE WORLD WHEELED ON.

The stars glistened above.

In the aftermath of the storm, the citizens closed their eyes, breath coming in long, deep draughts.

Not through sleep, though. Oh, no. Sleep wouldn't come to the citizens of the city. Not yet. Rather, their eyes clamped shut in primal fear of what was to come, the undeniable surge of rottenness that would alter their lives and make them question all that they thought they knew.

The tides were turning, and in the respite cast upon one shore, another must drown. As one stretch of sand welcomed the sea, another bade goodbye.

Such was the way of things.

A to and fro, balancing the karmic wheel. A storm must follow the drought. A spring must follow the winter. As surely as the sun must rise, it must also set, and allow the waxen moon its time to flex its rays and cast the world in the pixie glow of twilight.

A time when strange things happen.

When the unexplainable grow legs and walk.

When humanity shrinks its significance to that of a

grain of sand, and the monsters that lay hidden in the twisted fabric of reality find their cords and chatter.

A voice of a forgotten thing.

Channeled through the fluttering heart of a young girl.

A girl whose name was Juniper.

SHE STOOD on the brink of a broken thing, the edges of the stone slab, once razor-sharp, now dulled by weather and time to form only a small discomfort beneath her perfectly composed body.

The shakes were gone. In their place a quiet confidence, the girl's unblinking eyes staring down at the tarnished plaque set into the headstone. Words that once belonged to a mother, but which now belonged to a memory.

She hinged to her knees. Bony caps pressed against the forgotten earth. Weeds raised their curious heads toward her, keen to get a look at the starlit jar no longer crackling or dancing.

She reached a hand to the plaque, as if by tracing her fingers across the words she could feel her, smell her, hear her again. The warm embrace of a protective mother who once doted on her daughter. The scent of camomile and vanilla that permeated in the cotton of her clothing, tinged with the raw odor of a mother at work. The comfort of a mother's presence, swaddling her young baby against the dangers and wonders of the world, feeding her, watering her, teaching her offspring of love and life and laughter, of boys and girls and the correct way to cross the road. Imparting wisdom, sharing the ways of the first bloodfall, training the hand in cosmetics and arithmetic, encouraging Juniper on the countless days of school that were missed, time stolen, time snatched by a silent assailant in the throes of the night, a night such as this, when the blood moon soared high and the sickle was shaped for cutting, for killing, for thieving that which should have been better left alone...

Gone from this world.

Her mother. Stolen...

Juniper drew back her hand, head cocked, eyes dark with wonder. The bottled lightning waiting in silent anticipation, energy expended with each step taken toward the cemetery. The sharp cracks of activity dwindled until only a pool of liquid gold remained. The substance mixing with the dark grains of ash to create a viscous, gritty cocktail.

Juniper unscrewed the lid.

No lightning escaped.

She glanced in wonder, cheeks harshly shadowed by the illumination of the elixir, bones sharp like a polygon. Her skin pallid and drawn, waxen and sweating, the coat hanger smile stretching ear to ear revealing a maw interrupted with missing teeth.

She scooped a finger into the mixture.

It was warm, its energy traveling through her body, hardening her nipples, stirring warmth in the places she knew were forbidden, places she had feared to explore.

Her heart raced, a butterfly caught in a net. She swallowed dryly, turning the jar until the liquid pooled at its lip. She levered the container, allowing the gold to pour out in one fine string, soaking the base of the headstone.

The ground guzzled the liquid.

The liquid sought the cracks, fell down the crevices, sparked in sudden light, then faded.

Juniper waited.

The light faded.

The night silent.

She wasn't sure how long she waited for, statuesque and hauntingly still. The smile faded from her face as the moon arced across the sky and the sound of the world refused to return. Her eyes fixed to the headstone, her knees planted on the earth, weeds tugging the hem of her dress like animal claws.

The sky lightened. In the distance, far beyond the horizon, the first glow of morning gold peeked its winking eye. Juniper sighed. Rose to her feet. Turned.

Stopped.

A knock.

Another.

She turned back to the headstone, the knocking growing louder, bony fingers against wood. Juniper fixed her gaze on the headstone where golden letters spelled her name.

The earth rumbled beneath her feet. Juniper jumped back. Dirt shifted, a great mound breaching, a creature breaking its way to the surface.

An arm, sporting a golden watch with a chip on its face.

A shoulder, strong and round.

A crop of hair, snow-white and scraggly, fixed upon a withered skull, skin stretched balloon-tight across its face. A face she could identify anywhere.

The figure freed herself from the grave, rising until she towered over Juniper. Hazel eyes set back in hollow sockets. The threads of a cardigan she had received as a gift from her younger sister. A smile which broke the silence and returned the music of the world.

"Mom?" Juniper asked in disbelief.

"Baby..." her mother beamed, head tilting to reflect Juniper's own stance. Starlings sang overhead, their chorus rising as the wind whistled through the trees, and some-where, far off, the distant hum of traffic.

Juniper took a step toward her mother, then froze. Her mother raised a hand, taking a sudden step back. She cast her gaze around the cemetery. "What have you done?"

Juniper's heart stopped.

"What have you done!" A voice, harsh, shrill, and as cold as the missing years since Juniper's cradle.

Before Juniper could ask the question which clung to her tongue, a scream sounded in the distance. A harrowing, full-body, throat-destroying cry. A cry Juniper knew all too well as her own in the months preceding her mother's passing.

Juniper's brow beaded with sweat. She turned, noticing the ground vibrate. A headstone toppled and fractured, a lightning crack split across its breadth. Dirt loosened as another mound rose nearby.

"Mom?" Juniper asked, fear possessing her gaze.

Her mother leered back at her, eyes turned black, one bony arm reaching for her daughter's throat.

THOMSON AWOKE to a din of screams.

A raucous chorus, all singing off key, a dissonant choir of the damned.

He blinked the night away, unable to recall the moment he had fallen asleep. Across the mound of sheets that was Abigail, he saw that the beetle had taken flight, departed from its hollow. He supposed that was right. The work was done. His dear love departed from this mortal coil. Nothing more than a husk, a shell of what she had once been...

Something moved.

Thomson froze.

Something in his bed?

He called the dogs' names, but their barking came from downstairs. He looked beneath the sheets and found nothing, only the cold corpse of his deceased wife.

Cold...?

Yes.

Deceased...?

With trembling fingers, Thomson took Abigail's shoulder. He leaned across her stiffening frame until he could see her face. That same peaceful mask, her face a milky white in the darkness.

Two dark eyes staring back at him.

Thomson's screams joined the choir.

THE MOURNING VEIL

BY MARY RAJOTTE

There are no sweet nothings out here in the sugarcane fields. No one singing me to sleep in a place like this, where shushing sweetgrass whispers poisonous intent like a decaying lullaby. Here, there is only the overbearing shroud of humidity hanging over the Rio Grande Valley and a despair that seeps into every surface.

My single-wide trailer sits propped atop two concrete bricks on a ravenous patch of land where I camp with the other workers. It bulges at the corners like a waterlogged cardboard box, but I'm not sure if it's lopsided or if living hand-to-mouth keeps me off-kilter.

Sharp blades of moonlight pierce the row-crops that stretch up the cresting hill to Señor Morgan's farmhouse. In the air overhead, the sickly sweet tang of cut sugarcane stalks is a lingering insult, biting at my eyes and scratching my throat. As I leave the backbreaking day of work behind and go out into the grove of tangerine trees beside our encampment, I stare up at the spray of stars in the sky over the valley and find my escape.

"Oh, blessed Virgin," I whisper. "Madre María. Pray for

us, your beloved children. Help us walk valiantly through the sharp thorns in our path. Help us to one day return home."

But my voice gets swallowed by the silence out in the darkening night, and like cotton fibres, the wind takes my prayer and lifts it away before anyone hears.

At first, the shadows soothe, but when the air shifts, my scalp prickles at the sudden chill. Above me, a swarm, dark and wavering, approaches. The moths. They have found me.

As the murmuration ebbs and pulses in the distance, drawing nearer, the shadow-cloud silences the trilling cicadas in the trees. A thousand slow wingbeats find me in this place where I am anonymous to everyone but them. And like always, the moths won't stop until I acknowledge their message.

Each one is the size of a small bat and they come in a cresting wave, washing toward me. Some twirl in an unsteady dance. Others spin and flit around me until their wings skim a large puddle in the dirt. I go down on my knees and gaze into the dizzying patterns as an unending throng of moths falls like leaves to graze the water.

Swirling shadows flow together, intertwining into a silhouette that spreads like ink across the surface. Another moth touches the water, interrupting the image, changing the pattern into a mouth suspended in mid-scream. When the moths surge once more, they dive-bomb the puddle from all directions, battering it with their wings, pattering like raindrops until the cloud swallows the face whole.

Rising in an agitated upsurge, the moths leave as quickly as they came. I tap at the puddle, hoping to conjure the vision, but my touch only disperses the muddy water in dull waves. Grazing with my fingertips, I try again, but no magic surges to the surface, only grit and mold-mottled leaves.

Standing, I race to my trailer. Behind it, past the smoldering campfire where the other workers ignore sleep, past the cane fields, Señor Morgan's farmhouse, painted bright white, lurks like a hulking phantom on the horizon. Whether I am bent at the waist picking crops during the day, or tangled in my sweat-dampened sheets at night, it lingers on the periphery, always there, an inescapable menace.

I keep my eyes trained on it, as though looking away will allow it to creep closer, and I reach for my trailer door. Wind gusts behind me, pushing me sideways. I steel myself, but something slices my skin.

A moth lands on my bare arm, leaving raised bumps from its bite. The others race ahead, fanning out across the sky. They surge toward the farmhouse, drawing together mid-flight. Silhouetted against the moon, the moth cloud hovers in the shape of a flower over the house before blooming into a gaping mouth.

A cry chokes in my throat as I take off, tearing through the field. Cane leaves lash at my arms and legs, but I close the gap and make it to the farmhouse. Racing up the steps, I stop long enough for someone to clamp a meaty hand on my wrist.

"Don't you dare!"

Glaring, Señor Morgan's assistant, Sandalio, trains his one milky eye on me. Wet and jellied like the inside of a shucked oyster, it is as pale as a moonstone, the aftermath of the time last year when Señor Morgan lost his temper again and flicked his whip like a mare's tail, catching Sandalio off guard. I would feel sorry for him if he didn't treat us like he has forgotten he worked with us before Señor Morgan dressed him up nice and made him his servant.

"You saw them!" I say.

"You shouldn't be here, Marcela."

"I know you saw." I jerk my arm away, but he cinches his hand tighter, so I stand taller to keep him from dismissing me. "Another warning!"

"I didn't. Go on, now. Go home."

He spins me aside but before he can shove me, shushing like velvet rubbing together draws my attention overhead where the moth cloud unfurls, a dark veil spilling down around the house and swallowing it whole. The message is clear. Someone is going to die.

"Your stories put us all at risk," he says.

"These are not stories, Sando," I say, gesturing to the skies overhead. "You know what I see. You know my gift."

With a swift shake of his head, he denies everything about me, and it stings my heart.

"You should keep quiet and do your job," he says. "Like the others."

 "But the moths... their omen..."

"Enough!" he hisses. "Get out of here! And take your fantasies with you!"

I almost leave, but the way he snubs me only makes me more determined to have my voice heard. Staying quiet will only make the visions worse. And who am I if I don't stay true to our history of our people?

Since I was a child, the moths came to me, the same way they did for mi madre. For mi abuela. When I left behind everyone I love to come to this place, the moths didn't abandon me. They followed. Kept showing me things. Even though some—like Sando—are too afraid to admit their magic. There is coldness in his eyes. Even with what he knows, he will forever deny what he sees. But I cannot.

Pushing past him, I fling open the screen door and tear inside, leaving muddy footprints on the pristine cool tile.

"Señor Morgan! The moths have come back. I know what they are trying to say!"

Beside me, the parlour door opens. Cloying floral perfume and putrid sickness waft into the foyer. Wild-eyed and dishevelled in his vest and suit pants, Señor Morgan, the farm boss, brushes his hair smooth as I rush toward him.

"They've returned, Señor. The moths. They showed me. A blight is coming."

"Not this again," he says, his voice edged sharp.

"I saw it for myself. Sandalio! Tell him!"

Sandalio's jaw pulses, but he only shakes his head.

"There was a flower," I say. "Wilted and turned black."

He spins back to the small room where his wife, Iris, sits in a rocker with a blanket draped over her lap. Her eyes sunken in ghastly pools of crêpe paper skin, she presses a handkerchief to her lips and coughs. Thick phlegm rattles like stones in her throat.

"I helped to save the harvest before," I say. "Remember?"

"Enough," Señor Morgan says. He reaches for a small crystal trinket sitting on a sideboard near the doorway, as though it will distract him.

"I knew when Señora would become ill. Before her doctors, even," I say. "You believed me then. Why not now?"

"Enough!" He throws the crystal so hard that it clatters to the floor beside me.

I pick it up and hold it out to him, but Morgan ignores me, even though the truth he refuses to admit brings angry tears to his eyes. Lunging with his hands clenched together, his energy is a raging storm. I shrink from his wrath, but he only stands over me, pushing out his chest, his reeking breath sour from too many bourbons.

"I won't hear any more of these... these... visions of yours."

"But Señor—"

He backhands me so hard everything goes bright red. I am on the floor before I can brace myself for the impact.

"Sandalio. Take her."

Sandalio advances, but I push up onto all fours and crawl for the parlor door.

"You believe me, Señora. I warned you of your sickness. How the moths told me so. You thanked me! Remember? You have always been kind to me!"

A hand snatches me by the scalp, dragging me away from her. I howl, clawing at how Señor Morgan's fingers tear at the roots. I twist my body, but it doesn't stop him from yanking me outside, where he throws me down the stairs into the dirt.

"No more of this!" he shouts. "Sandalio! You have seen these moths?"

"Y-yes."

Señor Morgan looks out over the field. "Cut them down."

"Jefe?" Sandalio says.

"Whatever it is these moths eat? Cut every plant. Tear them from the roots. Starve them so they cannot come back. You hear?"

"No, Señor, please!" I cry, scrambling up to my knees.

He spins and lunges for me, swinging his arm, but stops short of hitting me. He glares, unblinking, the harsh moonlight etching long freakish gashes into his face.

"When you're done?" he says, his lips pulled tight in a

slash of a smile. "Burn the roots. Eradicate those bugs for good."

Sandalio turns and bolts away. He is halfway to the fields by the time I scramble up and chase after him.

"You can't do this!"

"Señor gave his orders."

"You know he is wrong. Por favor, Sando!"

"I listen to Señor Morgan when he tells me something."

I reach for his arm. "You remember how it was? When we first came here? They took everything about home from us when we crossed the border. You want to help them take this, too?"

He stops short and seizes my elbow. "Forget this, Marcela. These moths? They are not here to save us. They could never save a woman like you."

"I'm not the one who needs saving." I grab him by the collar the same way Señor Morgan likes to do. "You're one fancy shirt away from being put back in your place with the rest of us."

He turns and leans down so his fiery breath mists my face. "You hate him for having money. That is almost like him hating us for having none."

"They hate us for our skin, Sando! And they have made you hate yourself, too."

"¡Basta ya! Enough, Marcela!" He shoves me, marching past the beaten-down plot of land near the canals, far enough from the farmhouse that Señor Morgan doesn't have to see us every day. Past the encampment, he goes to the field where the moths settle high in the tangerine trees.

At first, you cannot see the oranges left to molder in the grass, but the overripe perfume makes my mouth water. Coming down from the treetops to feed in the moonlight, the moths are like a black shifting mass of bats supping the saccharine nectar from spoiled fruits.

Sandalio wades through them, punting the oranges away. Startled, the moths take flight, hovering around him, so he swats at them. I grab his arm before he can hurt them. When he swings to keep me back, the button keeping his sleeve tight at his wrist pops off in my hand, exposing his forearms, shrivelled with half-healed burn wounds. He pulls the fabric over the exposed skin and shoves me back.

"Doing this is hateful!" I say.

He spins and freezes, his eyes wide. "I do this to keep us safe."

"You spit on the memory of all of our people who came here before you! On their beliefs. And how the moths have been part of their lives, part of ours, for generations."

His nostrils flare as his ruined eye shifts and pulses with hatred. Striding forward, he stomps the discarded fruit with a squelch. I scream and tear after him, but he's already charging to a small patch of acacia plants where the other moths have taken cool refuge.

Taking up a machete left in an old stump, he attacks the plants. The blade *shinks* with each slice, lopping the leaves away, displacing the moths and battering some so badly they drop to the ground.

Screams from the other workers alert me to the crowd forming behind us at the encampment. Older women turn to bury their faces against their husband's chests. Younger men watch, mouths agape, at the sight of our history cut down, at the plants, so important to our people, taken so callously from us. Without the leaves, without the life-giving nectar, the moths will die and there will be no more.

"Sandalio!" Morgan's harsh voice cuts through the

group. He marches forward, one hand holding a gas canister, the other clutching a box of matches.

"No!" I say, rushing for Sandalio. "You can't! You wouldn't!"

"The things you people believe are just superstitious nonsense," Morgan says. "I won't allow it any longer!"

"Sando, please," I say, clinging to his arm. "Remember what the moths showed me. How your child would come early! I helped you, Sando."

"Enough!" Morgan tears the cap from the gasoline. Sloshes it across the carpet of squashed oranges and over the beheaded plants. Once emptied, he throws it aside and strikes a match, which he tosses at the base of the nearest tree. The fire leaps to life with an exhale that pushes us all back. Sandalio grabs me and pulls me away, but I claw to keep him at a distance.

Ignoring the carnage he has brought, Morgan stares me down, smirking, the flames leaping behind him before he brushes past and heads back to the farmhouse.

Beside me, there is a shout and a rush of activity. The men bring buckets of water from the camp, dousing the fire to stop it from reaching our homes. But it is too late to save the tree. It is a burning cross in the field, hatred ablaze against the night sky.

The moths lift away with wild abandon, lilting overhead like singed embers. Next to me, one falls in the grass. I kneel, cradling it in my palm. Its mottled blackish wings stretch from my thumb to my pinkie finger. Moonlight catches the thin bands of iridescent white threaded within each wing. But the moth goes still in my palm. I cradle her to me then tuck her into the pocket of my sweater, keeping her close.

At my feet, those too weak to escape gather in a heap.

The wind wafts the smoke overhead, an unseen hand renouncing the others from this place.

Up and over the fields, the moths flee in panicked flight. I don't know if it is the darkness as the fire dies out or the retreating swarm, but my vision fades like there is a shroud across my eyes. My hope wanes with it.

THE NEXT MORNING I wake with my skin, raw from last night's blaze, stuck to the bedsheets. The room is a haze of bright yellow and, when I blink, nothing comes into focus. Bolting upright, my insides seize with panic at the horror of losing my vision along with my foresight when Señor Morgan drove the moths away.

When I swing my legs to the linoleum, sticky with humidity, I stand and stagger sideways, woozily finding my way to the front door. I kick it open, shading my eyes from the harsh sunlight. Something dark shifts ahead of me and, as things fall back into focus, Sandalio's hunched shape paces in my direction.

"I know I'm late," I say, reaching for my hat and gloves on the stoop, but he takes me by the elbow before I can grab them.

"Come with me," he says, dragging me, his hand clamped so tight around my wrist that it burns.

"I will get to work if you only let me—"

"Señor Morgan wants to see you. Now."

He pulls me up the work road that bisects the two fields. When I stagger, he only yanks harder. By the time we reach the steps of the farmhouse, Morgan is at the top of the landing. Sandalio forces me up to face him.

"Have you seen anything new?" Morgan asks.

"Señor?" I ask.

"Those things. The moths. Have they shown you any of your visions since last night?"

My cheeks burn hot at the weight of expectation. "No."

He takes my hands and clutches them so tight my bones ache. "I need to know!"

"I'm sorry but—"

He yanks the door open and pulls me over the threshold.

"You said something about a blight. But you didn't mean the crops, did you? Did you mean my wife? What did they show you?"

"Por favor, Señor!"

"Tell me! Now! What did you see?"

"I can't. The moths. What you did... they are gone. They can't show me anything anymore."

He takes me by the scruff of the neck and shoves me into the parlor. Sheer drapes over the window filter hazy sunlight. Iris lies wan against her overstuffed bed pillows, the stale air around her thick and pungent like curdled milk. When Señor Morgan nudges me toward her, her eyes flutter open.

"She gets worse every day," he says, shoving me closer, holding me in place, forcing me to stare into Iris' bloodshot eyes. "You did this! With your talk of a blight! Look at her and see the sickness you've brought to this house!"

Iris' jaw twitches, but she is an immovable doll, her lips blistered and burned, pursed together, unable to speak. Her gaze darts to a rolling cart next to the bed. Her eyes widen, glaring at a glass water pitcher and then back to me.

"Where are your visions now?" Señor Morgan shouts, pushing me closer.

I want to tell him what I've seen, if only for Señora

Morgan's sake. But his demands cut too deep. Before this, he only ever ignored their message. Now, his desperation weighs too heavily. He forced Sandalio to cut the plants away. He burned the orange trees, not only to starve our moths but also to break our spirits. By taking something so sacred to us, he gave life to this dark cloud over all of us. The truth will only make his next retaliation so much worse for me, and for the others.

"I have tried to tell you, Señor," I say, trembling. "But—"

"Try harder! Speak!"

He grabs me by both arms, squeezing, shaking me. But in his glassy-eyed gaze, his anger has dissolved into fear. His determination tainted now by desperation.

Beside me, Iris coughs, thick and wet. I pull away and reach for the water to pour her a glass, but Sandalio lunges forward, knocking me into the cart. It upturns, spilling the contents to the floor.

"Enough of this! Get her out of here!" Morgan shouts, shoving Sandalio. "I'm a fool to believe in these so-called visions. If you can't tell me what I want to hear, then I'm done! With both of you!"

Sandalio wrenches me away, out of the house and down the steps, nudging me toward the road.

"Why did you do that?" I ask. "What was Señora Morgan—"

"Leave it, Marcela."

"I need to get my gloves first," I say, shaking from the confrontation. "And my hat."

"No. You're no use to me today. Go to your trailer," he says, turning away from me to look out over the fields. "But be ready to work twice as hard tomorrow."

As he leaves me there and makes his way to the fields already busy with the work of cutting sugarcane, I try to make sense of his words. This farm is so starved of kindness and compassion that this small gesture is as foreign to me as this place.

The guilt of getting out of my responsibilities for the day is a weight that gets heavier the further I pace away from the fields. But the other workers barely glance in my direction. It is as though the connection we have to one another has stretched so thin it will soon break, and that makes my heart ache more than any harshness I have to endure.

Back in my trailer, I hide in cool darkness. When my skin chills, I slip into my sweater, still smoky and sweetly citrus-scented from the fire. In my pocket, the fallen moth I rescued sits soft and unstirring. I remove her, placing her on the tabletop and stroke the delicate hairs on her wings, trailing my finger along the thin silvery bands, pressing my fingertips to her small spots. Outside, Sandalio's voice carries to me. Atop the crop truck, he stands barking orders at the workers. Every time he makes a demand, his harsh tone reminds me of how Señor Morgan would lash our backs and make us cut plants until our shoulders were in knots and our fingers bled. Sando, though, doesn't lead with a heavy hand. Instead, he brings out the floodlights to illuminate the fields, where he keeps command well into the night. After the work is done, the others return to their trailers, where their desperation suffocates the air around camp. None of us were born here, but we fight to survive, each reaping what we sow. Some do it by force, like Señor Morgan. Others, with harsh words like Sandalio. Only a bitter harvest can come from either.

I get lost in a haze of mourning, for the moths, for life back home, letting sweet heartache envelop me until the night settles deep. Then I wrap myself in my sweater and return to the orange field, to that place where Señor Morgan's hatred snuffed out the promise of our dreams.

In the meadow, the soot-stained wings of fallen moths lie abandoned, their delicate bodies shrivelled and black like liquorice whips. Gathering them together, I scrape back the soil around the destroyed acacia plants, creating an indentation. There, I lay them to rest, taking the frail moth I saved from the fire out of my pocket and placing her on top.

Sweeping the dirt over the grave, I notice a tall thin plant with small clusters of white flowers on the ground, cut down by Sandalio's rampage. They remind me of hemlock plants from my abuela's garden back home. Like her, I take care, using a leaf to pick up the shorn branch and place the blossoms on top of the mound.

The tiny treasures in my pocket weigh heavy with intention. The button from Sandalio's shirt. The crystal pendant from Señor's sideboard. A length of silvery thread taken long ago from Señora Morgan's sewing basket.

Taking two large twigs, I hold them together crosswise and tie them into a crucifix with the thread. The button, I fix to the center. The crystal I prop against the base after planting the cross in the dirt. With my hands clasped, I whisper a prayer that will sing my moth to sleep. One that will carry her back home, where I hope to return to one day. Then, bowing my head, I weep for all the things I have lost. My country. My family. My dignity. Here in this place, I feel more untethered than ever, grasping for those things that have been burned away and set adrift on the breeze, forever out of reach.

~

I VISIT THE GRAVESIDE NIGHTLY, but it isn't until a week later among the acacia remnants, dried and sun-scorched, rough-edged like sliced skin, that a tiny sprout, wispy as a feather, pokes from the soil.

Snaking across the top, the flowers from the hemlock plant have taken root and in the center, a thin membrane breaks the surface, silvery thread glimmering.

Pushing the plant aside, I dig the dirt away until I see the gossamer wings beneath. Still and unmoving, my heart sinks. But like a whisper, the air moves around me and a tiny flitting movement catches my attention. The soil shifts, falling in on itself as my moth comes to life.

Soon, more clamber to the surface. I lift them one at a time, helping them take flight before I turn back to the grave and free more who struggle in the heavy soil. Their wings are iridescent like stained glass, but my skin burns from their touch. Still, I help them, and they come together, blooming upward, outward, spilling across my palms and then flowing like water to the ground.

Like a slow-simmering flame, visions appear to me. The blistered skin on Sandalio's hands. Señora Morgan's burned lips and her panicked look at the water. How Señor Morgan tried so desperately to convince me I brought her sickness on myself. The moths and the visions they have shown me.

The glass pitcher.

The water.

I push myself up and as fast as my feet can carry me, I race for the farmhouse. Behind me, the moths follow, pushing me faster, ever closer.

On the front veranda, Iris sits propped in her rocking chair looking across the sugarcane fields. Señor Morgan is next to her. The glass is in his hands. At his lips.

"Señor!" I cry out. "Don't—"

Sandalio clamps a hand over my mouth before I can stop Señor Morgan, who drinks down the contents of the glass. He freezes, eyes bulging, his face burning bright red before he drops the glass to the veranda where it shatters at Iris' feet.

I break free from Sandalio's grasp and bolt up the stairs. Choking, Señor Morgan grabs me by the arm, his lips pulled into a deep snarl.

"You people think you can defy me? That anything you do matters?"

Foaming at the mouth, Morgan sputters, the sickness seeping between his teeth and spilling down his chin. Digging his fingers into my arm, he yanks me so close his sour breath mists my face.

"Each one of you is a blight that deserves to be buried and the earth over you salted so you'll wither away like those godforsaken bugs. When I'm done, you'll be a ghost. Forgotten garbage. Filth left to rot!"

He raises his free hand and prepares to strike, but before he can, the moths come together, descending on him, surging in a dark ribbon that threads between his lips, into his mouth, choking his hateful words. He doubles over, collapsing to his side, tears streaming down his cheeks. He flips onto his back, clutching at his throat as Señora Morgan cries out, clamping her hands over her mouth.

With his gaze fixed on Morgan, Sandalio doesn't move, only waits and watches Morgan's writhing.

"It was you," I say. "You did this."

Sando starts up, meting out each step before stopping beside me. "Only after he came to me, threatened to send me away, unless I would do the same thing to Señora, who has always looked out for me."

A handkerchief fallen to the veranda sits near my feet. I

stoop to pick it up and, taking Sandalio's hand, I press the cotton fabric to his palms, sliced with cuts from the hemlock branches, and blistered from touching the leaves.

"For us," I say.

Crawling forward, Señor Morgan wretches, his stomach contracting with each gasp. Seeing Sando's hands, raw with burns, Morgan's eyes go wide. When Morgan reaches to him for help, Sandalio doesn't move. Convulsing, shuddering, Morgan's fancy cowboy boots clatter against the floorboards. An ungodly noise starts deep in his belly and when he unleashes it, he spews the moths in a torrent from his lips. Gurgling, Morgan collapses, and when the breath finally goes out of him and the moths rise, he falls still, and at last, his oppressive presence is gone from this place.

I leave Sando alone, to comfort Iris, to tend to Señor Morgan, and I go down and out into the open field where the moths come together. At first, they remain brooding overhead. Then they drape down around my shoulders, obscuring my face, shading me like a mourning veil. They follow me down the roadway, past our camp, to the grove where we lost so much. There, the other workers are busy tending to my hiding spot, where, among the first new shoots of the acacia plants, more moths emerge from the dirt where I planted them.

Like us, they are fierce. Resilient. They have found some solace in this foreign place and rooted themselves here. As they lift and lilt in the air, their connection is not only to the land where they were born. Their magic is here and everywhere, all around, no matter how far from home they find themselves. No matter how far away they wander.

KNOCK ONE DOWN

BY KEVIN R. DOYLE

"Next block up," T-Ron said. "Just a little to the right. See 'em?"

Squinting into the sun, it took a minute to spot what the kid meant. A pair of large white sneakers looped around the electrical line stretched across the intersection. They dangled in the air like a sign of some kind.

"I've heard of this," I told T-Ron. "David mentioned something similar once. But I thought this kind of thing was in the past."

"In the past," T-Ron said, an odd note in his voice. "You mean before the storm?"

"Yeah," I said. "They still do this?"

T-Ron squinted into the fading sun, shielding his eyes with his hand.

"Not as common as it used to be, they say. But still happens. Whenever you see a pair of treads hanging like that, best to turn and go the other way."

It was something foreign to my own life. Tennis shoes looped around an electrical or phone line, or even a clothing line, held a definite meaning, at least in New Orleans. They served as a warning that you were about to enter enemy territory, similar to the prominently displayed shrunken heads that, according to every 1950s black and white Tarzan movie, marked the outer edges of a headhunter tribe's territory.

But it was a custom, so I'd been told, supposedly exiting the city around the same time as the vast majority of the population of the Lower Ninth Ward.

A custom, like most of the people, swept out of the city by Katrina.

"So the gangs are back to doing this again?" I asked, waving my hand in the direction of the marker.

T-Ron, who I'd picked up as a guide only a few hours earlier, shrugged.

"Not so much, these days. I don't remember any of that, you know. But according to what I hear, most of the boys left town with the storm, ending up in Houston."

While I didn't know his exact age, my guide looked to be no more than twelve or thirteen, which would leave him with no real memory of the hurricane that had nearly destroyed his home town.

"Did they stay?"

Another shrug.

"Some, I guess. Some didn't have a choice, got tapped when they took on the locals. A lot of them got rounded up by the cops."

"Houston cops?" I asked.

"Turned out to be a lot tougher than ours. Some of the boys weren't ready for how hard of a town Houston was.

Those that eventually came back"—shrug, again—"weren't quite the same as before they left."

"So whose shoes are those?" I wondered. "And how long have they been up there?"

T-Ron looked up at me, an entire universe of knowledge beyond my grasp floating behind those eyes.

"They've hung there long as I can remember," he said. "Ain't nobody going to mess with those treads. They belong to him."

"Who?" I queried.

"You know who. It's why you're down here poking around. Him."

BEFORE ARRIVING, I knew practically nothing of New Orleans. David, through various letters and emails, not to mention his occasional visits home, had provided me some cursory understanding of the place, but nothing, even pictures he'd posted online, had prepared me for the reality.

Nearly a decade after the storm that had so ravaged the Gulf, parts of the city, especially down in the Ninth Ward, still resembled a war zone. Not surprising, considering what it had gone through.

And as T-Ron took me on a tour that day, I had a hard time processing it all. Beyond the actual filth, the dirt caked into the walls of the houses left standing, we had to dodge broken pavement, exposed tree branches and rotted overhangs.

The people all had a haggard, hopeless look, as if nothing would ever work out for them again. I got lots of glares, and more than a few snickers, to let me know just how out of place I was down there.

At some point in that day, I began to wonder if finding out what had really happened to my brother was worth all of this.

"So you saw them?" Lindsay asked me later that night.

"Sure did. The kid took me right to them."

"He didn't try to rip you off, did he?"

"Naw. I may be new at this, but I was smart enough to not actually show my money until I was ready to part ways with him. Where did you find him, anyway?"

Lindsay shrugged.

"Around. Spend enough time down here, moving in and out of the various neighborhoods, and you meet all kinds of street kids. I've known T-Ron off and on for around four years now. Not sure where he lives or how much family he has, but he's one of those kids who always seem underfoot out on the street."

We were drinking wine at a small café on the fringes of the French Quarter. Fairly tall for a woman, Lindsay stood around five seven or so, and wore her red hair straight down to her shoulders. She also wore tinted glasses with almost non-existent frames, in an attempt, I speculated without hardly knowing her, to distance herself from the geeky academic she'd no doubt been in high school and college.

A friend and academic colleague of David's, she was nearly ten years older than me, and already beginning to show a little gray in her hair.

Then again, an associate professor at Tulane, she'd been doing cultural research in the city since before the storm, keeping up with it even after David's death, so one would think she'd be showing a lot of gray.

"Wasn't really that unusual," I said, yanking myself back to the main topic of conversation. "A pair of shoes dangling from some high wires. From what people say, that kind of thing used to show up on every other block down there."

"True," Lindsay said, pausing to sip her wine, "except for who those shoes supposedly belong to."

"Yeah," I said, feeling my voice starting to go remote. "I still can't really believe it, though."

"You don't think it's true?"

"You mean that there's an immortal gangsta who spends his time looking out for his little section of the Lower Ninth? Not hardly."

"Lots of confirmation to his existence, even if unofficial."

"According to the cops, High-Y is dead," I said. "They put him down the night the storm hit."

"But it could have been faked," she said.

"A dude nearly six-six in height? Armed with an honest-to-God Bowie knife? How could anyone have mistaken him for someone else?"

"Don't forget when he was gunned down," Lindsay reminded me. "That's as much a part of the story as anything."

"When they got him?" I asked. "Meaning what? The night the storm hit, or the night they say he gutted my brother like a fish?"

DAVID and I hadn't been all that close, not surprising with the age difference between us, but as a kid I'd pretty much hero-worshipped him. Trying to decide on either the military or college, he ended up going both routes, enlisting for a single hitch in the navy, then heading off to the university for a degree in criminology. Somewhere along the way, he hooked up with a group planning on doing some kind of intervention work with the drug gangs in the Lower Ninth Ward of New Orleans.

That's when my parents got worried, but at fifteen I just figured he was off on another adventure.

David spent his last weekend at home before heading down to the Big Easy, and even I could tell he wasn't his usual self. Between the slight facial tic, occasional staring off into the distance and only chuckling, rather than laughing, at our dad's best jokes, it was pretty obvious that he'd kind of changed his mind and wasn't really looking forward to his new work.

But heck, my bro had served on board a destroyer. How much more dangerous could this social research gig be than that?

A whole lot more, as it turned out.

"So when did High-Y's sneakers first appear on that wire?" I asked.

Lindsay finished off her glass and signaled the waiter for another.

"Right around a year after the storm," she said.

"When people began trickling back in," I said.

"You got it."

"But this High-Y character didn't trickle back in because he'd been killed on August 28, the night of the storm."

"Correct again. If the cops had been just a bit quicker, they may have saved your brother."

"You don't know that," I said. "Hell, far as that goes, we don't even know for sure that's how he died."

She looked at me. "Was it hard on you guys? Never finding his body or knowing for sure what happened to him?"

I didn't say anything, just sat there staring at the table, thinking of that one night that had haunted my family for the last decade.

~

HARD ON US? You could say that. Mom and Dad were freaking out over the news reports of the storm, trying like hell to get a hold of David. Remember, this was in 2005, and while cell phones were out and about, they weren't quite as ubiquitous as they are now. And even if they had been, it's doubtful that anyone could have gotten through to New Orleans during the last week of August of that year.

As the days and weeks mounted up, still with no word from their eldest son, my mom became even more unhinged. Dad ended up heading down there, vowing to go through every makeshift, temporary morgue and hospital in existence until he found his boy.

According to Dad, the local authorities were as sympathetic as they could be, but hell, they had just too goddamned much on their plate to deal with. With literally hundreds of bloated, disfigured bodies littering the streets, trying to identify one more was pretty much beyond them.

Eventually, he came back home, defeated and demoralized, leaving the three of us sitting around waiting for news that never came.

~

"You could say it was hard," I said, "but that wouldn't even be close. It took nearly a month for some of the people on your team to contact us, and all they had to give us were rumors from the street, things that sounded just too goddamned unbelievable."

"It was all the info we had to go on," Lindsay said. "David had kept us apprised, but those last few weeks, tracking down High-Y had become almost an obsession with him."

"An obsession," I muttered.

"Yes. He thought he had a shot at being one of the first people to pinpoint and confirm the origin of an honest-to-God urban legend, and by that point none of us could dissuade him."

I thought about that for a minute, but really couldn't think of anything to say.

"What did David tell you about him?" Lindsay asked.

"Not much beyond the basics," I said. "That there were stories about some sort of immortal thug who'd haunted New Orleans since before admission into the Union."

"That's all?"

"Well, that plus his theory that somebody, either in or out of the gangs, was keeping the legend going, planting evidence and spreading stories, as a way of protecting themselves. I know for sure that he never thought High-Y actually existed."

"Most of us never swallowed it either," she said. "At least until sometime after the hurricane, when we started hearing rumors about how High-Y had shanked David the night it hit. Before too long, it became practically common knowledge on the street."

"But no body was ever found," I said.

"No." Lindsay looked down at her wine glass for a moment.

"Lots of people never recovered after that night," she murmured.

~

ONE OF HIS emails started off:

> *How's it going, bro?*
>
> *Got to tell you, things are a lot tougher down here than you'd think. Even if you take everything the media says about how rough and corrupt this place is, and do it up ten times, you're not quite grasping it. Parts of this city, especially the Lower Ninth, are literally divided into tribal areas. It goes beyond the gang signs and boundaries of an LA, Chicago or St. Louis. This is even more brutal, in large part because of the cops. Whether because of low pay, being on the take, or flat-out incompetence, you have a couple of the housing projects here that even the SWAT teams won't enter.*
>
> *Can you believe that?*

~

I FLAGGED the waiter down and ordered another round for both of us.

"David said that this High-Y character was more of a myth than an actual person. That even in the heart of the Ward, few people would admit to ever meeting him."

"That's right," Lindsay said. "He was supposedly some kind of Lord High Enforcer of all the gangs. Working in the shadows to keep the peace among the factions."

"Judging by this town's homicide rate, he didn't do a very good job."

"Depends on your point of view. Lots of the Ward's residents thought if he hadn't been around, wherever he was, that things would have been flat-out carnage."

"But what I could never figure out," I spoke slowly, struggling to find the right words, "is how David managed to find him when no one else could, and what he wanted from him. You guys were down here doing academic research. Why the hell did my brother chase the lion into its den?"

Lindsay's face tightened, and a shadow seemed to pass across her.

"Because of our research, what we found out. I'm guessing, now, that David never told you?"

"Told me what?"

Lindsay tapped her fingers on the wrought-iron table for a moment, then reached into her purse and pulled out a folded-up piece of paper.

"This isn't an original, of course," she said as she unfolded, "it's a copy of a copy. The original's over a hundred years old and is kept in the library at Tulane."

She placed the paper, face down, on the table between them.

"Do you have any idea what the street name High-Y might have originally meant?" she asked.

"I've no clue," I said, "but if I had to guess I'd say it might be a reference to skin color?"

Lindsay gestured toward the paper, and I took it and turned it over.

It was a reproduction of an article from the *Time*

Picayune, and at first glance it seemed done in an old-fashioned script.

FREEDMAN SOUGHT FOR INCITING UNREST

The article, the printing kind of small and hard to read, told the story of a large Negro man suspected of causing some sort of ruckus among the newly freed slaves of Louisiana. The usurper was described as large, standing well over six feet tall, of a distinctly "high yellow" skin tone and wielding a Bowie knife against his enemies.

"High yellow," I said as Lindsay nodded. I took a closer look then, and felt everything inside of me begin to slow down.

"This isn't some sort of joke article, is it?"

"No," Lindsay said. "If you want, tomorrow I can take you to the university library and show you the actual item. I can also show you a few other artifacts, including some personal journals from around the 1700s that tell of a runaway slave hiding out in the bayous and making trouble for the slave owners. Same description, same knife."

I placed the paper down before me on the table, unable to take my eyes off of it.

The clipping was from March of 1867.

"This is why David took the chances he did," Lindsay said.

"You mean he thought that the person in this article was the origin of the legend?"

"No, Chris. David thought High-Y *was* the person in the article."

~

THE SIMPLISTIC VIEW of New Orleans, at least pre-Katrina, depicted a holdover of the antebellum South. The romantic French Quarter, a few plantation mansions remaining in the old section, people dawdling through lazy days in the humid southern summer. Jazz music and liquor at night, Mardi Gras raising the roofs each spring.

The truth was always something different, and along with so much property, money, and life, Katrina, not to mention Rita coming along about a month later, swept away a lot of the illusions.

The people of the town, especially the poor, never held those illusions, and for most of them, at least those who managed to return, the back-to-back hurricanes only made clear to the outer world what they'd always known.

Yes, Nola did have the ornate balconies, the cobble-stoned streets, the women flashing for beads during Carnival, and all the rest.

But the city, as my brother had discovered during his time here, also held other, darker, and more ancient elements.

Elements such as High-Y.

The taxi, which picked me up on St. Charles Avenue, just outside of Tulane's main campus, dropped me off about ten blocks from the abandoned tenement I'd visited the day before. The cabbie absolutely refused to go any closer to the now renovated projects, and I could tell that he was looking for some way, without bringing up my skin color, to dissuade me away from whatever errand had brought me to this section of town.

I paid him off and walked away, ignoring his final protestations.

It was the middle of the morning, the sky rather overcast, the breeze bringing with it a hint of moisture, cleanliness, from somewhere beyond the Ward.

Another illusion, one of the last few I was desperately trying to hold on to.

This time, I didn't stop half a block away. The street looked deserted, though I pretty much figured it wasn't. Nevertheless, using the sidewalk I strode right up to the electrical wire which held High-Y's shoes. The shoes that had marked, not his drug territory, but his shelter, his haven.

One of the other pieces of information Lindsay had given me the night before.

~

"THAT'S INSANE," I told her around about our fourth glass of wine. "There's no way David would have believed anything like that. He wasn't stupid."

"'Course he wasn't. He was one of the brightest people I'd ever known. And don't ask me how he got onto it, because I have no clue. But I think you misunderstood me."

"I hope so," I said, "because it sounds like you said that my brother believed some kind of gangbanger in the twenty-first century was actually hundreds of years old."

"See," she said, "probably my fault for not making it clear. I didn't mean that David thought High-Y from the projects was the same man who'd led the insurrection after the Civil War or the old slave from before that."

"No. So what did you mean?"

"David had the idea, and if it was right he was rather brilliant, that someone was deliberately fostering that image, doing their best to make the urban legend seem true."

"To what end?" I asked. "What good would it do anyone to try to pull something like that off?"

"That's what your brother was trying to find out," she said without looking at me, "when he was killed."

I'd always imagined the phrase "skin crawling" for just a figure of speech, at least until I approached that old building. Standing right under the sneakers, looking all around me for any sign of another person, I could literally feel a hundred sets of eyes on me, untold numbers of the local residents probably just waiting to see what would happen to Whitey.

I hadn't asked Lindsay to come along with me this morning, seeing no reason to put someone else in jeopardy. And when I'd tried to contact T-Ron, willing to offer him more money just to give me some protective camouflage, he wouldn't answer.

But I had to know. My life had been on hold for nearly a decade, ever since David's death.

The disappearance, and probable murder, of their eldest son had torn my parents down to nothing. In the furor after the storm, in the near unbelievable carnage and chaos, they never found David's body. Lots of stories, about how the street thug known as High-Y had slaughtered him in one of the back alleys, but no real proof.

Then again, David never did return home, and as far as his university buddies could determine, the rumors were more or less true.

My dad began drinking even more than he had previously and, before my eyes, he turned into a raging bigot, a regular Archie Bunker. Or maybe he always had been, and only now realized he had nothing to lose by expressing his opinions of anyone of a different color than him.

And my mother?

Mom just kind of collapsed in on herself, stopped caring about what she looked like, what she ate or what anyone thought about anything. Never the most outgoing of people, she became almost a complete hermit. She quit her job and spent all her days and nights just waiting for Dad to come home from the nearest bar.

I'd done my best to build a life for myself. Sports in high school, then on to a decent college. Had a couple of serious girlfriends, though never one that stuck around for too long. Eventually, I took up drinking, just like dear old Dad, and ended up just drifting from one low-end job to another.

The month before, I'd lost my latest job, and this time something kind of snapped inside of me. I figured it was time, once and for all, to make as much sense as I could out of the senselessness of David's death.

So I sold my car, cashed in a couple of loans from friends, and headed down to the Big Easy. Although it took a little bit of knocking around to find David's old colleagues, slowly but surely I got on his track.

Which led me to here.

NOT ENTIRELY A SURPRISE, the edifice was as deserted as it appeared. At least of human life.

But as soon as I stepped across the threshold, I could hear the scurrying and slithering of all sorts of lower forms.

The building had probably been on its last legs even before Katrina, and I figured the structure must really be in bad shape if no one had bothered to move in, even informally, in the years since.

Or, I wondered, did those dangling shoes really have the power to keep anyone, no matter how desperate, away?

I paused just inside, listening. Aside from my own harsh breathing, and the aforementioned slitherings and scurryings, I didn't hear much of anything.

I moved to the staircase along the far wall, my feet partially sinking into the spongy wood. The early morning humidity, plus the lack of ventilation in the closed-up building, already had my shirt sticking to my chest and back.

A fear of splinters, not to mention whatever had been there before, kept me from placing my hand on the stairwell, causing me to go slower than normal as I headed up, testing each riser as I went to ensure its solidity.

About halfway up, a stair riser creaked below me.

I stopped motionless, not turning around but listening as hard as I could. I heard no more creaks and wondered if some sort of animal was wandering around, frozen into immobility by my own stillness.

Finally, knowing I'd have to sooner or later, I turned and looked back down the way I'd come.

A man was standing on the third riser from the bottom.

The only light in the building came from outside, wending its way through various gaps and rends in the walls, but it was enough for me to see him rather clearly.

Tall fellow, really tall. I couldn't tell, looking at a downward angle, if he reached the mythical six foot six, but he probably came close enough that it wouldn't make a whole lot of difference.

Broad shoulders and probably a narrow waist, though

with him wearing a baggy sweatshirt, the sleeves cut off, it was hard to tell. But those cut-off sleeves revealed a pair of massively muscled arms, one of which held a big, ugly blade.

Definitely a lighter-skinned Negro, the kind that, in a less politically correct time would have been called high yellow, from which he no doubt got his name.

He held the blade at a partial angle, not leveled though clearly in my direction.

I couldn't find a trace of emotion on that face, as expressionless as a piece of wax.

"You're not a ghost," I said, "a ghost wouldn't have made noise on the stairs."

Still showing no expression, the figure began waving that long, nasty silver blade back and forth in front of him.

He no doubt intended the move to terrify me, and it was having the desired effect. But I'd come this far, halfway across the country and over a decade in time, and no way would I back down now.

I had to know, dammit. I had to know the truth of David's death.

"They call you High-Y," I said, my words seeming to momentarily hang in the tenement's stillness before dropping off into non-existence. "And they say you've patrolled this area for a long time."

The rhythmic sweeping of the blade stilled for a moment, then began again, infinitesimally faster than before.

"There's stories of a large man, light-skinned, involved in the Prohibition business during the twenties, enforcing the boss's kill orders. And I saw a reproduction of a newspaper story from just after the Civil War, about an upstart high yellow Negro terrorizing the carpetbaggers."

He tilted the knife up in a vertical line, holding it about shoulder level before sweeping it back down. My eyes stung with sweat, but I didn't dare blink.

"And everybody thinks you're the same one. My brother came down here, right before the storm, looking for you. He had it figured out, that someone, or maybe several some-ones, was keeping the myth alive. That's right, isn't it?"

For once, a break in that impassive face, a slight smile just as the blade did a figure eight in the air.

"And he found his proof, he must have, which is why you did him in. Well, not you, but the one before you. So what's the deal? How many of you have there been? Going how far back?"

I felt as if I was babbling, which only made me babble even more. But, somehow, I had to do two things.

I had to get the truth out of the enigmatic figure down at the bottom of those stairs, and I had to get out of there.

The knife stopped moving, remained frozen for a moment, and the man took another step upward.

This time, the riser didn't creak.

"What I don't know, and can't figure out," my voice by now had risen to a near falsetto and I had to fight to get it under control, "is who's behind you? Who could have had the necessary resources and foresight to keep something like this going for so long?"

Then a voice sounded, not below from the giant, but behind me, at the top of the stairs.

"You are one stupid white man," it said.

I whirled and saw T-Ron standing about six risers above me. Only now, he didn't appear as a helpful, generous kid just wanting to earn a buck.

Now he looked hard, his eyes soulless, a gangbanger in training.

"Wha..." was about all I could get out.

"Shit, man. Where you think you are? Don't you know this is Nola? Don't you know anything about what they say about old-time folks around here? Huh?"

It took me a minute, but then I thought I got it. I couldn't believe it, but it was the only thing that made any kind of sense, no matter how warped.

"You're talking about voodoo? You saying High-Y is some kind of zombie?"

The kid laughed, his mirth sounding like a merciless bray.

"Voodoo? What the fuck kind of fool are you, white? This is something a whole lot older, a whole lot deeper. Goes all the way back, farther than anyone knows. And you still ain't getting it. Look at High-Y there, take a good look at him."

A bit leery of turning my back on the kid, I nevertheless half turned and looked back at the being down below.

Except now he wasn't below anymore. Somehow, without any notice or sound, he'd made it to just two risers removed from me which, with his height, put us almost on eye level with each other.

"Take a good look at him, white. Voodoo? Zombie? That's the biggest joke of all. Look at him. This is his territory, his domain to keep. And ain't nothing, no slave whips, no Klan lynching, and no blue with his nine that's going to drive him away. Look at him close. And if you still don't get it, you completely hopeless."

By that point I wasn't listening to the kid because I'd already seen the familiarity. Not in the body, of course, nor in the height. Not in the color, naturally, or in anything about the facial features.

But in the eyes.

I knew those eyes. I'd known them my whole life.

But I hadn't seen them in nearly a decade.

"David?" I whispered, so shocked that I wasn't sure I spoke at all. Behind me, T-Ron began laughing again.

"Knock one down, another comes up. He just keep going and going and going. What you think about that, pale?"

I didn't answer, couldn't answer.

I had nothing left to say as High-Y's blade sliced into my body.

MELTHAM'S CHILDREN

BY CHRIS MOSS

To: ashfield.caroline@dcsph.gov.org

Dear Dr Ashfield,

It was good to make contact with you too, although your request was somewhat unexpected. Yes, I am familiar with the global phenomenon of Meltham's Children—how could I not be? The deformities first described by Meltham have been a scientific conundrum for almost twenty years, occurring across social, racial, and geographic lines.

Astronomy is hardly a related field, but I too find myself wondering if the aberrations are the result of a critical mass of toxins in the environment or whether it was a biological weapons test gone awry.

In answer to your question, I have no idea why the "children" under your care keep gathering on rooftops on certain nights of the year. However, I hardly see the point in wasting observatory resources looking at a patch of blank sky.

I will admit, I'm impressed you were able to calculate the coordinates based on such basic observations. It seems you haven't forgotten everything I taught you.

I don't want there to be any bad blood between us, so rest assured that this polite refusal is based on the university's policy, not out of any childish sense of wounded pride. If you do insist on grasping at straws, please file a formal research project with the university.

Sincerely,
Dr Clark Denton

If this email has been sent in error, please contact university administration.
Coming soon! 2046 Collegiate symposium "The Challenge of Meltham's Children: Toward a reorganization of Nation States." Details to be provided.

∼

To: den.clark@unra.edu

Dear Dr Denton,

Thank you for your prompt reply. Honestly, Clark, you don't need to be so formal—everything's fine, really. As for my request, I'll file a request on behalf of the government, but I'm assuming the university will recognize that my department can hardly requisition a deep space telescope on their own.

As for the Meltham's Children (and yes, I'm aware that a

significant proportion of them are no longer children), I think you've missed the point. I've been working with them for years. They're all people living with the same physical deformities, the bloated glands, the gray skin, the modified throat and eyes. There are further mutations across different groups, but genetically they are all essentially the same. I know that the focus has been on how the mutations started —at least by the governments who survived the public frenzy, but I think there's more here than just ensuring we can have "normal" births again.

I think the children are intelligent.

I know they don't speak, or write, but when you've spent as many years with them as I have, you get a... sense, I suppose. Like these little unspoken rituals, the gatherings on certain times of the year. We've had linguists listen in at every audible frequency, body language experts analyze every microexpression, but so far they've turned up zilch.

There must be more going on. Eventually, all these children will be adults, and we will need to make space for them in our world. Before that happens, we need to be able to communicate. If I can find out what they're all so fixated on, it could be the key to opening up some real dialogue.

Stay in touch, Clark. You have a brilliant analytical mind— and I still think of you as a friend.

Dr Caroline Ashfield, Project Officer
Department of Community Safety and Public Health

DCSPH—Fostering stronger communities through wellbeing and togetherness.

AppAudioLog20460307

AshCa: Clark, you've heard?

DenCl: Yes. I'll admit, the results were pretty surprising. Looks like you didn't need that requisition after all, The Tripartite States got to it first.

AshCa: It's a star, Clark. Right where they were looking. You can't deny a connection! Now do you believe me?

DenCl: Stop being so dramatic, Caroline. There's any number of celestial bodies in that direction. These so-called children could have been staring up at anything. And, for what it's worth, it's not a star, it's a comet. Probably dragged in from the main belt. The chance of it getting within a million kilometers of Earth is less than winning the lottery. We don't need to start howling at the moon like the mobs out on the street.

AshCa: I'm not a Restitutionalist, or a Neo-Monarchist, or any of the others, Clark. Don't be so damn arrogant. Have you been out on the streets lately? We've got militias armed to the teeth saying it's a sign from God that they should take over the country, conspiracy nuts saying the children are a secret government experiment, and Alt-Nazis forming hit squads so that they can "purify the gene pool." The department has had to round up as many of the Meltham's Children as we can find before something happens to them!

DenCl: Perhaps something should happen to them.

AshCa: Clark, that's disgusting! They're *people.* People like you and me, who are living with a genetic condition. You can't dehumanize them. If you got out of your ivory tower, you'd see that.

DenCl: Caroline, they're not human. You can dance around the semantics all you like, but we all know it's true. Every double-blind genetic study has confirmed it; there's no way that these mutations could have reasonably occurred, simultaneously, across so many populations. You want to ask *me* to get out of my ivory tower? Have you *seen* what's happening? It's not just a handful of governments being toppled, we have entire nations completely incapacitated by the burden of caring for these "children." Hell, most young couples are terrified of starting a family in case we produce another generation of monsters!

AshCa: Don't go there, Clark. Don't you dare bring that up.

DenCl: Why shouldn't I? You don't want to admit it, but this was part of the reason we broke up, wasn't it? You can assuage your guilt all you like by playing Mother Teresa to these creatures, but at the end of the day you were just as scared as the rest of us that we might give birth to something hideous.

AshCa: Damn you. You have no idea how hard that decision was for me. You can't judge—it's not the same for men and you know it. To have something growing inside you and then find out how different it can be? I was terrified, Clark. There—does that make you happy? I was so scared of my own womb that I could barely function. That still doesn't mean that we get to collectively discriminate against a global population of people. Especially one that might have some kind of communication and organization that's beyond us!

DenCl: Why? Because they stare at the sky? Ascribing them intelligence that they just don't have, out of pity, doesn't help. It doesn't change a single damn thing out there in the real world.

AshCa: Fuck you. Don't contact me again.

Transmission ended.

~

To: ashfield.caroline@dcsph.gov.org

Caroline, are you there?

Please contact me, I need to know you're safe.

Caroline, I understand if you don't want to reply, but if you are getting this, find shelter.

I shouldn't be telling you this, but the rumors are true. This comet... there's something wrong with it.

Sincerely,

Dr Clark Denton

If this email has been sent in error, please contact university administration.
Following the SoE declaration, the university campus is closed indefinitely. All students are encouraged to stay in their homes until further notice. For more information on safety and survival, visit the university portal.

~

To: den.clark@unra.edu

Clark,

It's alright, I'm safe. I'm sorry, I should have told you my email changed when my Executive Directors announced the Department was being reorganized. The government has gathered most of us up into an emergency facility outside of the insurgency zone. I can't go home, not yet, but I've got solid walls around me. Are you ok?

What is this comet, Clark? I still remember a few bits and pieces from our uni days, and I know it shouldn't change direction like that.

Do you know how much time we have until it hits? Amateur astronomers, celebrity tubers, conspiracy nuts, they're spreading photos of it over the net. Hell, some people are calling it the "Red Cataclysm," they're tattooing themselves and attacking government facilities. People are saying they're crazy. They are. They're nuts.

Have you been having weird dreams, too?

It's probably just the stress.

I'm sorry we parted on such bad terms. You're still important to me. I just want to know you're safe.

Caroline.
Department of Emergency Operations and Disease Control (former DCSPH).

For a full guide to community safety, please visit the department's website. DEODC urges your cooperation with army deployment personnel.

To: ashfield.caroline@deodc.gov.org

Caroline, I'm so glad you're safe. I've been terrified one of those bastards got to you. Stay where you are, the government facility is the most secure place in the city.

I'm ok, the university gave instructions months ago. I'm already sick of canned tuna and beans, but as long as the water stays on, I'll manage. The apartment block is barricaded, and I've done my best to nail the door closed. Remember that time we tried to build a bookcase? Yeah, it looks just as bad.

If I keep my lights off no one looks twice at my apartment. But what I've seen, Caroline... it's horrific. The streets below are a running battle between different factions. I have to hide when the Doomsday preppers turn up to loot the shops, but most of the other groups don't have guns. They all disappear in the evening, though. The comet is just a red smear during the day, but it's blazing at night. That's when the cultists come out.

I have, honestly, no idea at this point. They're mad, plain and simple. They scream and sing and paint red symbols all over their bodies. I think they're the ones who burned down the Church the next block over. Maybe they're having the dreams too?

Please stay safe. It's all gone to hell and I couldn't bear it if you were hurt.

I'm sorry I was so cruel before. I do hate them. I can't help it. They took you away from me and nothing's gone right in my life ever since.

Please stay safe. I need you.

Clark

If this email has been sent in error, please contact the sender of the email.
The university warns that rioters will be met with deadly force.

To: den.clark@unra.edu

Clark, thank God, I thought I'd lost you. Please stay safe. Don't come out of the apartment block, no matter what. Is

there a basement in your building? It's thick concrete, right?
You need to barricade yourself in there as soon as you can.

I wish you were here, Clark. The government science offi-
cers are screaming at each other in the halls—they think I
don't know what they're going on about, but I recognized a
few of the words from our time together. "GCR"—the R
stands for radiation, doesn't it? This star, or comet, or whatever it is, it's broken off into chunks. There're dozens of fragments circling the globe, radiation boiling off every piece,
and it's falling toward us.

We're safe for the moment. There're soldiers in HAZMAT
suits everywhere, I think they're worried about what will
happen to the atmosphere once the comet hits. Society may
have to go 1950s nuclear bunker and live underground for a
generation.

I can't sleep, Clark. These dreams—we're all getting them.
Something is coming. Something unnatural. The children
are feeling it, too. Most of our facility is now given over to
trying to keep them under control. The closer the comet
gets, the more agitated they become.

They caught one of the scientists yesterday, out in the yard
when they are allowed up to get some fresh air. He was
trying to get some blood samples. I've never seen anything
like it, Clark. The way they moved, wordless, but with
perfect coordination. They rounded on him, herded him
away from the door, then attacked. They're growing stronger
and stronger. When I screamed at them to stop, that he was
just trying to help them, do you know what happened? They
turned and looked at me, Clark. For the first time, they actu-

ally engaged when someone communicated with them. All of them, at once. They all turned their heads in perfect unison and looked at me with those black eyes.

I'm scared, Clark. I don't know what's happening anymore. Please stay safe. Get underground. I don't want to lose you either.

Caroline
Department of Emergency Operations and Disease Control (former DSPCH).

DEODC strongly recommends citizens shelter in place. Further instructions will be provided.

AppAudioLog20460714

AshCa: Clark, are you getting this?

DenCl: Caroline! Are you ok? I saw the news report. Please tell me you're safe.

AshCa: I'm safe for the moment. The military is on-site, they've pushed the cultists back out of the breach. They're insane. Mad. A dozen cultists must have killed themselves in the initial blast, then the rest came pouring in through the hole. Clark, listen to me. When the cultists got in, the children got out.

DenCl: I don't understand? The cultists freed the children?

AshCa: I don't know, it all happened too fast. All I saw was that the moment these tattooed freaks got into the walls, the children were there. There were screams, fighting, but the children ploughed through them like they weren't even there, then left. They were moving in perfect coordination, Clark. I need to find out why.

DenCl: Caroline, no! What are you doing? You haven't left the facility, have you?

AshCa: The facility is no longer safe, Clark. I took one of the HAZMAT suits and I'm following the children.

DenCl: Please! Please get back into the facility, into a bunker, anything! The radiation is already reaching dangerous levels. Wherever these comet fragments are, whatever effect it's having on the Meltham's Children, it's not worth dying for!

AshCa: It's so red, Clark. It's all dark crimson, the sky, clouds, the dust. There're corpses everywhere.

DenCl: You'll be one of them if you don't find somewhere safe!

AshCa: The children are moving faster. I can see their bodies through the dust. There're thousands of them. Thousands and thousands. They're moving toward the center of the city. They aren't being affected by the light, did you know that? Something in their makeup? Genetic. Must be. Their glands, their eyes. They're fine.

DenCl: *You're* not! Damn you, Caroline, I can't do this without you. Look, you were right about the children. They are intelligent. They must be. They're simply something we don't understand yet. We can work on opening up communication with them together, I promise, just please, get away. If you can't go back to the facility, come to my apartment block. I can find a way to block the worst of the radiation, break the barricade seals. I can let you in. Don't leave me.

AshCa: It's so bright now, Clark. You can't imagine it. Everything is black but the sky is on fire. The children... they're all around me. They're looking up. Waiting.

DenCl: Damn you, Caroline! Listen to me!

AshCa: It's here, Clark. It's just like my dreams. The stars are dripping with blood and falling from the sky. It's above us now, it's... It's...

DenCl: Caroline!

AshCa: ...it's *unfurling.* It's not a comet, Clark. Never was. It's... I can't find the words. It's hideous. Beautiful. It's wings and arms and eyes.

DenCl: *Caroline!*

AshCa: So many eyes, Clark. White and Red, reflected in the black of Meltham's Children. They're—Clark!

DenCl: Please, my love. Please. Come back to me. I'm sorry I doubted you. *Please.*

AshCa: They're attacking, Clark. They're fighting it. Whatever *it* is. The noise. *God!* I can't stand it. It's too much. I can't move, Clark.

DenCl: Please.

AshCa: I understand, now. I get it. They wanted me to witness this. They wanted me to see. They're dying. Hundreds of them, torn to pieces. Silently falling around me. But they're still fighting for us. All this time, they knew. They *knew.* They must be fighting across the globe. Fighting against the Red Cataclysm.

DenCl: Caroline, listen to me very carefully. I need you to snap out of this. Walk away and—

AshCa: I think it's too late, my love. The radiation tag is already beyond the danger point. This close, the HAZMAT suit might as well be tissue paper. Do you know what? All this time, we thought they were some kind of aberration. They're not. They fit perfectly here.

DenCl: Please...

AshCa: They're not out of place in this new world, my love. We are. And if we are very, very lucky, they may make room for us.

Transmission lost.

THE SPLIT THROUGH THE SKY

BY LENA NG

First published in "Hinnom Magazine," Issue 010, 2019

An evil has tainted my sleep. More than night terrors, what skin-crawling, defiled, and heaving abominations have come to plague me in my dreams. Body twitching and seizing until, in the dead of night, my eyes flung open, overstretched, to stare despairingly through my bedroom window into the endless, dark night canvas. Instead of stars, the pinpricks of light seemed as holes where an unknown, unfathomable voyeur was spying from the other side of the nocturnal sky as through a camera obscura.

The second night, horrors most urgent bled from my ears. The insectoids scurried beneath the thread-bare blankets and scuttled over my skin. Nightmares made phantasmagoria crawled through my orbits to tattoo scarification patterns on the insides of my eyelids. The patterns mimicked the unsettling pattern of the stars.

The third night, a humanoid people in blasphemous

tongues mutter-intoned in my sleep. They pointed at me and drew a star pattern in the dirt. Beyond their goatish eyes and snouts, some strange familiarity in their facial features, primordial ancestors in my reincarnated past danced and gestured an obscene beckoning to join them.

Before I had gone to bed on the first night of torments, I had noticed a disturbing alignment of stars. According to mathematics, stars and planets should follow a predictable elliptical path. But the planets of Versiveus, Kraelov, and Diaxon moved in enigmatic, unnerving voyages. Other stars crossed in horrendous formations, and I quaked at what such signs could mean. Though seers, prophets, and oracles read portents in tea leaves, in the scattering of bones, in the twist of lines on palm, I could read warnings in the positioning of outer planets, the fleeing of corrupted stars, and the burning of Azurrabed's comet, their bizarre and unpredictable movements in the black canvas of the cosmos not foreseeable by any astronomer or scientist.

Nor had my dreams contained the usual symbols and images of falling, fleeing, or flying. The fragmented glimpses of mesentery-moist, pulsing, flesh-like megacilia could mean a multitude of ambiguities and insinuations and I fled to the underground libraries for answers. The cowled, tongueless monks accepted my bodypound and I smelled the burning of my sacrifice as I followed the silent shroud of the monk deeper into the labyrinth of tunnels. He performed the crucial signs, sang the voiceless canticle, and the vault doors to the Deep Room, notched with protective rites, clanked open.

Franticly, feverishly, I delved into the delirium-inducing *Mortemordis*, poured through the curse-riddled *Gorgonology* using antidote-laced gloves, and studied the abhorrent *Maledictory*. Even locking myself in a fetid room with the

Almanac Enigmata, the poison book of knowledge, could not answer my questions. I left when I began to weep blood.

Back in my studio, page after page I flung to the floor as I drew diagrams, scribbled equations, created derivatives and reductions of the movement of the stars, knowing the patterns of the celestial formation must be part of a grander design. Not the math of this world but the math of the parallel: non-Newtonian geometry, Fortunado's topology, octrine trigonometry. Not even the black calculus of Crucerbus could decipher the malevolent pattern.

After weeks of haunted nights, tired and with a suffocating blanket of dense depression which ground down my bones, I paid a visit to my great uncle, my only living relative though I had not spoken a word to him since I had finished my studies. Both my parents had died when I was a child and this secluded great uncle funded my upbringing and education. He was a gray, morbid man, his skin a pool of wrinkles, his frame seemingly stirred by a thread of will which animated his body like a puppet. I told him of the primeval people who beckoned me to join them, the foreboding alignment of the stars, the flash of animal-human hybrids that mutilated their fleshy forms in profane ways. When I spoke of these horrors, his face blanched as though he had seen the unnamed visions, the impure inferno, the contaminated images conjured before him.

He knew this day would come, he had told me. He had read the signs. He had heard it in the crow's screech, saw it in the psoriatic cirrocumulus clouds, and he trembled beneath the ominous stratocumulus sky.

He arose from his sunken chair, and from a gold chain around his neck, he pulled forth a twisted key like that of a skeletal finger. He used this key to unlock a base metal box, carved patterns on its sides like a demonic hellish puzzle box. From his box he took out a yellowed ugly leathery papyrus that, I came to realize, was made from human skin.

"Here," he said as he thrust those papers away from him into my hands, "your real name."

As I opened the dried wrinkled skin paper, the unclean hieroglyphics undulated on the page, no letters in any human language decipherable. With this unpronounceable name came papers outlining my adoption at birth. This explained the remoteness of the parents I had known, Fabien and Magdalene Vigilius, so distant growing up, so lacking in warmth and parental affection. They were instead my gatekeepers, my guardians, my family of strangers. I played alone, ate alone as my parents watched as distant silent observers. However, my true ancestors, the ancestors of my dreams called to me.

Upon retrieving the documents, my great uncle sank back into his chair. He said, "You were adopted through the Gentrocide agency, in Blackheart, New England. They may have more revelations for you." After he uttered these words, it was as though his purpose had been completed and he collapsed, shrunken into a desiccated corpse before mine eyes.

BLACKHEART, New England. From my research, a barren hamlet with abandoned decrepit buildings set like battered teeth on salted, charred earth. Once a rural village in the late seventeenth century surrounded by crops of squash, beans, and corn before a Puritan offshoot religion grew more extremist. Medieval extraction techniques such as foot roasting, hamstringing, and denailing led to confessions of the practice of blood sorcery. The accused were executed by hanging, burning, and drowning.

So much innocent blood was spilled on the land that it ruined the earth, and guilt and insanity drove out the remaining settlers. Over the years, new colonists, looking to return to the old ways in a fundamentalist folly, would try to settle the land for another rebirth of the village. But the befouled land could not sustain the population and the settlement would eventually die again. It was during one of these resettlements that the Gentrocide Orphanage came into existence.

Before undertaking a trip to this sinister locale, I decided to investigate other methods to delve into my twisted, enigmatic roots. I swabbed my cheek to give samples to genealogy decoders, to find if I could unravel my family tree through the secrets within the coding of my cells. They mapped out my genes. Long strands of deoxyribonucleic acid formed helical patterns of adenine, thymine, guanine, and cytosine. But, shockingly, other nitrogen bases, nonhuman ones, were also identified: dendrosine, parnadrine, lytonine, and monomotomine.

The scientific methods could not determine my heritage. Long segments were marked inconclusive, or nonhuman, but no explanation could be ascertained. Twenty-nine percent unknown ancestry. No relatives traced on the cyber genealogy tree.

If I am not fully human, then what am I? Resurrected through recombinant gene-splicing? Hybridal chimera, part human, part nightmare?

∽

BY PLANE, by train, and by foot, I made my journey, my driver quick to surrender me alone to the thick forest when he read a road sign citing "The Path of Righteousness." By compass and coordinates I would find my way to Blackheart. The shivering woods were gloomy, dark and deep, and the crows screeched themselves hoarse against me in the descending light. The scuffle of my feet on dead leaves sounded as though I were a monster stalking the woods.

My knapsack weighed heavier on my shoulders the longer I trudged through the woods. Despite the thickness of the forest canopy, without urban light, I saw clearer the unexplained calibration of the stars and felt naked beneath them.

It was close to dawn when I reached the outskirts of an outcropping of a dozen buildings, the decaying village of Blackheart. Nature had reclaimed the land. Vines of ivy tangled an insidious stranglehold over the crumbling stone buildings. The makeshift roads were empty and long weeds pushed through the crumbling paving. The silence was empty and it seemed to be everywhere.

A copper-green plaque by the door alerted me to the Gentrocide Orphanage. The orphanage looked as though built as an old brick church, a morose, lachrymose building. Four windows with faded black shutters stood guard on either side of a black-painted door. The door creaked as I opened it. The interior of the building seemed colder than the exterior, a psychic as well as physical cold, and breath transformed into apparitions. Charcoal shadows seemed burnt into the walls, as though an atomic bomb had detonated and blasted the shadows from the occupants. When I listened closely, I could hear a faint scratching emanating from behind the aging plaster. Likely rats or other vermin, and I had no desire to discover its inhabitants.

In a logical manner, I would start from the second story of the building and work my way downward. Vile moisture ran down the walls like a sickly sweat. The breathy sounds of scurrying centipedes under watchful spider eyes. Glowing, disembodied stares seemed to follow my every move as I wound my way up the rickety staircase to the upper level.

The door to the first room already stood open. It was a large rectangular room with three rows of empty cribs. The walls were painted a cloying green, peeling in some spots, large lace-like splashes of mold on others. The suffering of the prior inhabitants infused the walls, the atmosphere. My imagination, or at least I hoped it was only the imagination, heard the ghostly crying of children.

The next room held hole-ridden, rotting furniture where termites and wood-borers feasted. A writing desk, a splintered chair, and five filing cabinets set against the mold-splashed walls that sent up clouds of rancid dust as I went through their contents. The wood broke as I yanked the locked desk drawer open. A box, which I dashed upon the floor, contained yellowed leathery papers with slash-marked hieroglyphics.

When I touched these papers, the house began to creak. A loud wailing sound swept through the house and the floor beneath my feet began to shudder. The walls bulged rhythmically, as though a giant wormy heart had awoken within the plaster.

I fled the building as though a pack of demons pursued me.

~

I FELT as I had brought home a curse. The slash marks danced on its yellowed skin, and no matter where I was in my house, I felt its malignant presence. At night, it whispered venomous secrets that crept on the edge of consciousness. The mutterings infected my dreams. In my night's visions, the stars grew brighter, larger, and seemed to sprout teeth.

I sought audience with the highest professors of the Occult University, linguistic savants of the opaque, unspeakable languages. The University, a brutalist monolith, was hewn from stone and ornamented with petrified blackwood. The rooms were star-shaped, and through the bending of the other dimensions, there were an infinite number of them. The mosaic flooring resembled the waves of the ocean, burgeoned with unnamed creatures, and the ceiling was patterned with stars.

The twelve monks grew silent as I brought forth the yellowed page. They burned cleansing herbs and chanted obsessively in an infrasonic language before touching the document, but even then there were no guarantees of protection.

Finally, after much consultation through incantations and incense, oratory and arguments, they referred me to High Priestess Narinka, a cleric who lived in the ruins of an Oracular temple in southern Notambishi. She had foreseen the death of the New Redeemer, the outbreak of the white pestilence, and the first wave of the Third Coming, the horrors from which had struck her blind. But her sight with the third eye, the eye which sensed the reality beyond, grew exponentially more powerful, a sense that had grown more acute from the loss of another. She had no age; she was as old as time. She suffered no fools, however. Many fortune hunters, if they had not perished in the journey, had been driven mad in her presence. Four monks, having reached the upper echelons of euphorical meditation, and armed with binding amulets, agreed to take me to the site.

Seven days we spent climbing up mountainside where the air was thin and altitude sickness had us bent and gasping. Seven days bitten by insects the size of our palms, leaving eye-sized welts. One monk developed a sweating sickness and died after convulsing. Another disappeared one night, deep in the middle of Mandire's Forest, presumably abandoning the journey.

At last, we reached the stone steps at the mountain's peak leading to her temple. I joined hands with the remaining monks and repeated their incantations before we took the first step. They continued their chanting until we reached the top of the stairs, blanketed by fog. The red columns of the temple were engraved with prayers.

The High Priestess's face was round and smooth, with a cupid-bow mouth, mask-like in its serene perfection, with a cluster of eyes that took up much of her forehead.

The two remaining monks' droning chant rose in volume. I took out the yellowed document from my bag, prostrated onto my knees, and pushed the paper toward her. The eye cluster glowed with a pearly sheen. She brushed the tip of her foreleg against the leathery paper. She split her mouth open and lightly tapped me with her mandibles which had extruded from within. I tried not to tremble under her arachnid caress. A thin, curved fang pushed out and pierced me through my cheek. She tasted the drop of blood using a long pink tongue.

"Yesss," she hissed, "so now is the time." The eyes turned upward to the sky. "You are the catalyst, the key to the door. Go to the place of your birth. Follow the River Aox until you find its source."

She watched me as I stood. I backed away from her.

When I reached the stairs, I fled. The blood had whetted her appetite and she took one monk as an offering.

THE PLACE OF MY BIRTH. The River Aox, a holy river where local people believed that bathing in its waters would free them from the cycle of life and death, grew narrow and more winding as the last monk and I followed it upstream. The thick forest gave way to long grasses and tangled, rope-like vines the width of my wrist. Finally, we were met with an abattoirial circular stone inscribed with hieroglyphics.

As the monk stepped onto this formation, the atmosphere grew oppressive and bristled with warning. A slicing sound cut through the air. The monstrous vegetation, with its tendrils, lashed around the final monk until he looked spooled as a ball of twine. The living jungle pulled him by the limbs into the sky. In a whiplash, the vines retracted, the speed of which cut into his skin. He fell onto the stone and bled to death before me, a death by thousands of cuts, the stone absorbing the blood.

I ran but there was no need to pursue me. The tendrils snapped around and dragged me to the circular stone. From there the vines retracted and from the lashes flowed my blood. Instead of crimson, the fluid glowed with an ominous phosphorescence. At its taste, the stone beneath me splintered, the sound thundering in my ears.

Above, the dark sky cracked open, and from this eggshell split, an unnatural infernal octrine light, a vomitus yellow-green from the deep outer infinity of the cosmos, shone through. Masses of squirming, pink-fleshed appendages, glistening moist from the universe's mucosal lining, thrashed their way twisting through the split, like an eruption of monstrous worms in a radiation pit. Cup-shaped mouthparts rhythmically suctioned open and shut while hordes of giant tick-like parasites scuttled over the organ-raw mass.

My eyes couldn't encompass the horrific imageries. The vitreous liquid contained within my eyes boiled, and from the toxicity of the visions, the eyeballs burst within the sockets, scorching the scarification tattoos beneath my eyelids. I should have been blind, but the octrine-vile light opened my third eye, the eye which allows us to see into the multiplicity of dimensions and I was cursed with a hideous knowledge.

The translated letter described how I was meant for slaughter. The code lay in my cells, my blood, the key pattern to opening this hellworld with the proper alignment of the stars. I was born to be sacrificed to the Ancient Ones under a bleeding moon in the center of pentagonating stars but was snatched away by the remnants of a fundamentalist missionary sect.

Now with the stars above once again in formation, the spilling of my blood the key, I saw the gibbering slave-priests, my dream-kin who had called to me in the unconscious nether realm, grovelling in eternal madness to the gods Goreth, Ramsire, and Baphthmotet. Commonly known as The Triumvalent, the Unhallowed Trinity, from whom our human concoction of Satan or the devil is but a weak facsimile, the true entities infinitely more evil, infinitely more conflicting, delighting in destruction and in everything which is in opposition to the good and righteous. Its spirit is encompassing, infecting all parts of human nature, so we ground down those already fallen into the dust. My blood ushered in the new world as I was tormented in hideous helplessness upon a fractured altar.

Above, an acidic sticky toxin rained down and burned raw holes in my body. The smell of sizzling flesh contaminated the air. Outpoured forth from the widening split in the sky hailed vast monstrous creatures—deities—from the nether-dimensional realms. The flaming, long-toothed Snakehead... the chimeral, dual-tongued Lizardwalker... the hoofed, unbounded Goatman with the split, weeping eyes...

ABOUT THE AUTHORS

Warren Benedetto writes short fiction about horrible people doing horrible things. His stories can be found in anthologies from Scare Street, Black Hare Press, and Devil's Rock Publishing, in publications such as Dark Matter Magazine and 365Tomorrows, and on podcasts such as Tales to Terrify and The Creepy Podcast. He studied Evolutionary Biology at Cornell University, and has a Master's degree in Film/TV Writing from the University of Southern California. When he's not writing, he works as Director of Global Product Strategy at PlayStation, where he holds 20+ patents for various types of gaming technology. He is also the developer of StayFocusd, the world's most popular anti-procrastination app for writers. He built it while procrastinating. For more information, visit www.warrenbenedetto.com and follow @warrenbenedetto on Twitter.

An award-winning teacher and writer, **R.A. Busby** spends her spare time running in the desert with her dog and finding weird things to write about.

A member of the Horror Writers Association, Busby's story "Street View" (Collective Realms #2) was recently selected for the Preliminary Ballot List for the Bram Stoker Awards for 2020. Other published horror stories include "Bits" (*Short Sharp Shocks* #43), "Holes" (*Women in Horror Anthology #2: Graveyard Smash*), "Cactusland" (*34 Orchard* #2), "Kiss" (Women in Horror Anthology #3: *The*

One That Got Away), and "Baby" (*Good Southern Witches Anthology*, forthcoming).

A high-school teacher, former college instructor and fiction writer, **Kevin R. Doyle** is the author of three crime thrillers, The Group, When You Have to Go There, and And the Devil Walks Away, published by MuseItUp Publications, and one horror novel, The Litter, published by Night to Dawn Magazine and Books. He also is the author of the Sam Quinton private eye series. The first two books in that series, Squatter's Rights and Heel Turn, have been released by Camel Press. Doyle teaches English and speech at a high school in central Missouri.

Julie Hiner spent endless hours during her childhood lost in books. The only thing that took precedence was her Walkman. Julie is still a hardcore 80s rocker at heart.

Julie secured a solid education and career in computer science. She switched paths to finish her non-fictional book, an inspirational story of facing fears, cycling, and massive mountains.

Fuelled by a long-time fascination with the dark mind of the serial killer and inspiration from a talk by a local homicide detective, she flung herself into writing her first novel. She now runs KillersAndDemons.com – Tales of Dark Crime and Horror.

An ex-touring, professional musician, **David Ivey** gave up his rockstar dreams of traveling the world, opting to settle down and marry the love of his life. It was a wise choice. Together they have three children, lots of love, and an incredible home life in Atlanta, Georgia.

Though David still plays the occasional concert, his

passion for writing allows him the fulfillment of an innate desire to create something worth enjoying, all while being the father his kids deserve.

David is currently working on his first novel, anticipating its release late 2021.

For more, you can find David at: www.davidiveywrites.com or Facebook.com/davidiveywrites

Leeroy Cross James is a horror writer from Cheshire, UK. His short stories have been published in anthologies and adapted by horror narrators on podcasts and YouTube Channels. Leeroy's non-fiction work includes articles for Horrified Magazine and Horror Oasis. He currently studies English Literature and Creative Writing at John Moores University in Liverpool.

Find more from Leeroy on Twitter: https://www.twitter.com/ZombiLeeroy, and Instagram: https://www.instagram.com/leeroycrossjames/

Zoltán Komor was born in June 14, 1986. He lives in Nyíregyháza, Hungary. He writes surreal short stories and is published in several literary magazines (Wilderness House Literary Review; Drabblecast; The Phantom Drift; Gone Lawn; Bizarro Central; Caliban Online; Bizarrocast; Thrice Fiction Magazine; The Missing Slate; The Gap-Toothed Madness; Kafka Review, etc.) and anthologies (Unity, Volume 1: A Magical Realism Charity Anthology benefiting Doctors without Borders; The Horror Collection: Emerald Edition, etc.).

His first English book, titled Flamingos in the Ashtray: 25 Bizarro Short Stories, was released by Burning Bulb Publishing in 2014, his second English book, titled Tumourdjinn was released by MorbidbookS in the same year, and his third collection, Turdmummy was released by Strange-House Books in 2016. In 2020 his short story titled "Mall-Head" won The Monolith Prize in Hungary.

An award-winning author and professional archaeologist, **Chris Moss** has worked with museums and historic sites, and currently spends his days wandering the bush tracking down old ruins. Inspired by his travels through the word's great heritage places, Chris's stories explore men and women caught up in the demands of their own history. When not at work, Chris enjoys board games and dancing around the house with his wife and three daughters.

Lena Ng roams the dimensions of Toronto, Ontario, and is a monster-hunting member of the Horror Writers Association. She has curiosities published in close to sixty tomes including Amazing Stories and the anthology We Shall Be Monsters, which was a finalist for the 2019 Prix Aurora Award. Her 2021 upcoming publications include The Half That You See, Polar Borealis, Love Letters to Poe, Selene Quarterly, The Gallery of Curiosities, Green Inferno, Dread Imaginings, Ghost Orchid Press, The Quiet Reader, Bone-yard Soup, The Needle Drops, Dark Dispatch, Cosmic Horror Monthly, The Ghastling, Murderous Ink, and Sage Cigarettes. "Under an Autumn Moon" is her short story collection. She is currently seeking a publisher for her novel, Darkness Beckons, a Gothic romance.

A resident of Toronto, Canada, author **Mary Rajotte** has a penchant for penning nightmarish tales of folk horror and paranormal suspense. Her work has been published in works from the Library of Horror Press, the Great Lakes Horror Company and Burial Day Books. Mary is a member of the Horror Writers Association and was the recipient of the 2018 HWA Scholarship. Sometimes camera-elusive but always coffee-fueled, you can find Mary at her website http://www.maryrajotte.com and at patreon.com/maryrajotte for exclusive fiction

Daniel Willcocks is an international bestselling author and award-nominated podcaster of dark fiction. He is one fifth of digital story studio, Hawk & Cleaver; co-founder of iTunes-busting fiction podcast, 'The Other Stories';' CEO of horror imprint, Devil's Rock Publishing; and the co-host of the 'Next Level Authors' podcast.

Dan is furiously passionate about all things story. He has written 40+ books in four years for himself and on behalf of ghostwriting clients. Dan's author coaching services are designed to help authors take the stories that they are dying to tell, and getting them out onto the page. Find out more at danielwillcocks.com

OTHER TITLES BY DEVIL'S ROCK PUBLISHING

Novels

When Winter Comes (Collected Edition)

Serial Fiction, "When Winter Comes"

The First Fall (Episode 1)

Buried (Episode 2)

Black Ice Kills (Episode 3)

Masks of Bone (Episode 4)

Into the White (Episode 5)

Winter Comes (Episode 6)

Anthologies

The Other Side: A Horror Anthology

Keep up-to-date at

www.devilsrockpublishing.com

www.ingramcontent.com/pod-product-compliance
Lightning Source LLC
Chambersburg PA
CBHW020802190726
48285CB00006B/2139